Horatio Alger

The Backwoods Boy

The boyhood and manhood of Abraham Lincoln

Horatio Alger

The Backwoods Boy
The boyhood and manhood of Abraham Lincoln

ISBN/EAN: 9783337735029

Printed in Europe, USA, Canada, Australia, Japan

Cover: Foto ©Raphael Reischuk / pixelio.de

More available books at **www.hansebooks.com**

BOUND TO WIN LIBRARY

This library is "bound to win" its way into the heart of every American lad. The tales are exceptionally clean, bright and interesting. PUBLISHED EVERY WEEK.

THE BOUND TO WIN SERIES—Continued

The Backwoods Boy

OR

THE BOYHOOD AND MANHOOD OF ABRAHAM LINCOLN

By HORATIO ALGER, JR., *author of "The Erie Train Boy," "Luke Walton," "Adrift in New York," "The Store Boy," "The Young Outlaw," etc. . . .*

STREET AND SMITH, PUBLISHERS
238 WILLIAM STREET, NEW YORK

l

PREFACE.

I VENTURE to say that among our public men there is not one whose life can be studied with more interest and profit by American youth than that of Abraham Lincoln. It is not alone that, born in an humble cabin, he reached the highest position accessible to an American, but especially because in every position which he was called upon to fill, he did his duty as he understood it, and freely sacrificed personal ease and comfort in the service of the humblest. I have prepared the story of Lincoln's boyhood and manhood as a companion volume to the life of Garfield, which I published two years since, under the title, "From Canal Boy to President." The cordial welcome which this received has encouraged me to persevere in my plan of furnishing readers, young and old, with readable lives of the greatest

and best men in our history. I can hardly hope
at this late day to have contributed many new
facts, or found much new material. I have been
able, however, through the kindness of friends, to
include some anecdotes not hitherto published.
But for the most part I have relied upon the well-
known and valuable lives of Lincoln by Dr. Holland and Ward H. Lamon. I also acknowledge,
with pleasure, my indebtedness to " Six Months
in the White House," by F. B. Carpenter ; Henry
J. Raymond's " History of Lincoln's Administration," and the " Life of Lincoln," by D. W.
Bartlett. I commend, with confidence, either or
all of these works to those of my readers who
may desire a more thorough and exhaustive life
of " The Backwoods Boy."

HORATIO ALGER, JR.

NEW YORK, *July* 4, 1883.

CONTENTS.

Lincoln, about twelve years old. Leaning against the cabin in a careless attitude was a tall, spindling boy, thin-faced, and preternaturally grave, with a swarthy complexion. He was barefoot and ragged; the legs of his pantaloons, which were much too short, revealing the lower part of his long legs; for in his boyhood, as in after days, he ran chiefly to legs.

Who in the wildest flight of a daring imagination would venture to predict that this awkward, sad-faced, ragged boy would forty years later sit in the chair of Washington, and become one of the rulers of the earth? I know of nothing more wonderful in the Arabian Nights than this.

The second boy was a cousin of the other two children—Dennis Hanks, who, after the death of his parents, had come to live in the Lincoln household.

The sun was near its setting. It seemed already to have set, for it was hidden by the forest trees behind which it had disappeared.

"Abe," said the girl, addressing her brother, "do you think father will be home to-night?"

"I reckon," answered Abe laconically, shifting from one foot to the other.

"I hope so," said Dennis. "It's lonesome stayin' here by ourselves."

"There some one comin' with father," said Nancy slowly. "We're goin' to have a new mother. I hope we'll like her."

"It'll seem good to have a woman in the house," said Dennis. "It seems lonesome-like where they're all men."

"I reckon you mean yourself and me," said Abe smiling.

The boy's grave, thin face brightened up as he said this in a humorous tone.

"Then I ought to be considered a woman if you two are goin' to set up as men," said Nancy. "But Dennis is right. It'll be good for us if she's the right sort. Some step-mothers ain't."

"I reckon you're right," said Abe again.

"I'm afraid she won't like the house," said Nancy. "It ain't as good as it might be, though it's better than the 'camp' we used to live in."

As she spoke her eyes turned toward an even more primitive dwelling forty yards away. It was known as "a half-faced camp," and was merely a cabin enclosed on three sides and open on the fourth; built not of logs, but of poles. It was fourteen feet square, and without a floor. Here it was that the elder Lincoln lived with his family when first he settled down in the Indiana wilderness after his removal from Kentucky. The present dwelling was an improvement on the first, but how far it was from being comfortable may be judged from a description.

It was indeed a cabin, while the other had been only a camp, but it had neither floor, door, nor window. There was a doorway for an entrance, but there was nothing to keep out intruders. There was small temptation, however, for the professional burglar. The possessions of the Lincolns were altogether beneath the notice of even the poorest tramp. A few three-legged stools served for chairs. In one corner of the cabin was an extemporized bedstead made of poles stuck in the cracks of the logs, while the other end rested in the crotch of a forked stick sunk in the earthen floor. A bag of leaves covered with skins and old petticoats rested on some boards laid over the poles. Here had slept the elder Lincoln and his wife, while Abe laid himself down in the loft above. A hewed puncheon supported by four legs served for a table. A few dishes of pewter and tin completed the list of furniture.

This was the home to which Thomas Lincoln was bringing his new wife. She was a widow from Elizabethtown in Kentucky, where he had formerly lived. She was an old flame of Mr. Lincoln, but had rejected him, being able, as she thought, to do better. But when within a few years he became a widower and she a widow, the suit was renewed and the answer was favorable.

Even now the married pair are on their way home.

Mrs. Johnston considered herself a poor widow, but she was much better off than the man she had just married. She was the owner of a bureau that cost forty dollars; this alone being a value far greater than her new husband's entire stock of furniture. Other articles, too, she had, including a table, a set of chairs, a large clothes chest, cooking utensils, knives, forks, bedding, and other articles.

"Look, Abe!" said Nancy in sudden excitement, pointing to an approaching vehicle.

Abe followed the direction of his sister's finger, and he opened his eyes in astonishment. A large

four-horse team was in sight—a strange and unusual spectacle in that wilderness. The children
could not have been more excited if Barnum's
grand procession of circus chariots had filed into
view—a vision of Oriental splendor.

"There's father!" exclaimed Abe, distinguish-
ing with a boy's keen vision the well-known figure of his father sitting beside the driver.

"Father and Uncle Ralph," corrected Nancy.

"And the team's full of furniture Can it be
comin' here?"

"I reckon your new mother's aboard," said
Dennis.

This remark made the children thoughtful,
because it recalled their own sad-faced and gen-
tle mother who had faded from life a year before
and gone uncomplainingly to her rest. Then,
besides, the prospect of a step-mother is apt to
be disquieting when nothing is known of her dis-
position or character.

"Is all that furniture comin' here?" solilo-
quized Nancy wonderingly.

"I reckon so," answered Abe.

When the team came nearer another exciting
discovery was made. There were others aboard

the wagon besides their father, their new mother, and their uncle Ralph Krame, who was the owner of the team. There were two girls and a boy, children of Mrs. Lincoln by her former marriage. They were not far from the same age as the three children who were awaiting their arrival, but they were much better dressed. It was clear that the log-cabin would no longer be lonely. It would be full and running over. The six children and their parents were to be crowded into it.

"That is my house, Sally," said Thomas Lincoln, pointing out the cabin in the woods to his new wife.

"That !" she exclaimed in dismay, for her new husband had led her to expect that he was tolerably well-to-do, not with any intention to deceive, but mainly because they had different standards of comfort.

We can imagine that the heart of the new wife must have sunk within her as from the wagon she caught the first sight of her future home. She had not been accustomed to luxury, but her old home was luxurious compared with this.

She relapsed into silence, and did not choose to make her husband uncomfortable by revealing the true state of her feelings. She seems to have been a capable woman, and probably made up her mind upon the instant to make " the best of it." Besides, she had already caught sight of the children.

" And those are Nancy and Abe?" she said.

" Yes," answered Thomas Lincoln. " That's Abe with the long legs, and the other boy is his cousin Dennis."

The new Mrs. Lincoln regarded with womanly compassion the three neglected children, and in her heart she resolved to make their lot more desirable. Perhaps the children read her face aright, for, as they scanned her kindly face, all fear of the new step-mother disappeared, and they responded shyly, but cordially, to her greeting.

CHAPTER II.

THE NEW MOTHER.

WHEN the new Mrs. Lincoln entered the humble log-cabin which was to be her future home, it may well be imagined that her heart sank within her at the primitive accommodations, or rather, lack of accommodations.

"How do you like it?" asked Thomas Lincoln, who was much more easily satisfied than his wife.

"Not at all at present. There are no doors or windows. There is not even a plank floor."

"We have got along without them," said her husband.

"We can't get along without them any longer. You are a carpenter, and can easily provide them. I will put in my furniture, and after awhile we will have things more comfortable."

"I don't think we need the bureau. You say it cost forty dollars. You had better sell it. It is sinful extravagance to have so much money in furniture."

"I can't consent to that," said Mrs. Lincoln decidedly. "I have nothing that is too good for us. I will see that you and the children live more comfortably in future."

Abe and Nancy looked on with interest while the bureau and the other possessions of their new mother were taken from the wagon by their father and their uncle Ralph. They began to think they were going to live in city style. In particular they admired the bureau which had cost forty dollars. Why, their cabin had not cost that. They felt something like the country minister of sixty years since, to whom his parishioners presented a carpet for the "fore room." When it was spread on the floor, he gazed at it admiringly and ejaculated, "What, all this and heaven too! This is too much!"

Mrs. Lincoln was quite in earnest, and set her husband to work the next day at the improvements she had specified. When after a time they were completed; when the earthen floor was succeeded by one of boards; when two windows had been set in the sides of the cabin, and a door

closed up the entrance; when the primitive bed
and bedstead had been superseded by the new-
comer's comfortable bedstead and bedding, and
the three-legged stools had been removed to give
place to chairs, the three children were very
happy.

And indeed it was a happy day for Thomas
Lincoln and his young family when his second
wife took charge of his household.   She was
kind-hearted and energetic, and though she had
three children of her own, she was never found
wanting in care or affection for her husband's
children.   She took a special interest in young
Abe.   She read him better than his father, and
saw that there was that in him which it would
pay to develop.

To begin with, she rigged him out in new
clothes.   His ragged condition had excited her
sympathy, and she rightly judged that neat attire
helps a boy's or girl's self-respect.   I have no
doubt that Abe, though he never had a weakness
for fine clothes, surveyed himself complacently
when for the first time he saw himself respecta-
bly dressed.

This is the description of Abe's step-mother

given many years after by Mrs. Chapman, the daughter of Dennis Hanks :

"His wife, my grandmother, is a very tall woman, straight as an Indian; fair complexion, and was, when I first remember her, very handsome, sprightly, talkative, and proud ; wore her hair curled till gray; is kind-hearted and very charitable, and also very industrious."

It may be mentioned here that this good lady lived long enough to see the neglected boy whom she so kindly took in hand elected to the highest place in the gift of his countrymen.

It was not long before Mrs. Lincoln began to broach her plans for the benefit of her step-son.

"Abe," she said one day, "have you ever been to school ?"

"Yes, ma'am. I went to school a little while in Kentucky."

"You didn't learn much, I suppose ?"

"Not much ; I can read and write a little."

"That's a good beginning. In this country, Abe, you will never amount to much unless you get an education. Would you like to go to school?"

"Yes, " answered the boy earnestly.

"I will speak to your father about it. Is there any school near here?"

"Yes, Mr. Dorsey keeps school about a mile and a half from here, near the Little Pigeon Creek meeting-house."

"You and Nancy and Dennis must go there.'

Mrs. Lincoln broached the subject to her husband.

"Abe ought to go to school, Thomas," she said, "and so ought the other children."

"I don't know as I can spare him," said his father. "I need his help in the shop and on the farm."

"He can find time out of school hours. The boy must have an education."

"I agree to that, wife. It shall be as you say."

In Mr. Dorsey's school Abe's studies were elementary. His time was given to reading, writing, and ciphering. The school-house was about as primitive as the Lincoln cabin before the improvements were made on it. It was built of unhewn logs, and holes stuffed with greased paper supplied the place of windows. It was low-studded, being barely six feet high. The scholars studied in classes, and Abe's ambition was ev-

cited, so that he soon came to be looked upon as one of the foremost scholars.

A year or two later, in the same humble school-house, a new teacher named Andrew Crawford wielded the ferule. He was, it may be inferred, a better scholar than Mr. Dorsey, and was able to carry his pupils further.

Abe was now in his fifteenth year, and was growing at an alarming rate. He was already nearly six feet in height, and must have pre-sented a singular appearance in the rustic garb in which he presented himself at this temple of learn-ing. I quote Mr. Lamon's description of his phys-ical appearance and dress :

"He was growing at a tremendous rate, and two years later attained his full height of six feet four inches. He was long, wiry, and strong ; while his big feet and hands and the length of his legs and arms were out of all proportion to his small trunk and head. His complexion was very swarthy, and Mrs. Gentry says that his skin was shrivelled and yellow even then. He wore low shoes, buckskin breeches, linsey-wolsey shirt, and a cap made of the skin of an opposum or a coon. The breeches clung close to his thighs and

legs, but failed by a large space to meet the tops
of his shoes.. Twelve inches remained uncovered
and exposed that much of 'shin-bone—sharp, blue,
and narrow.' 'He would always come to school
thus, good-humoredly and laughing,' says his old
friend, Nat Grigsby. 'He was always in good
health, never was sick, had an excellent constitution, and took care of it.' ''

It impresses us rather curiously to learn that
the new teacher Crawford undertook to teach
"manners" to the rough brood that was under
his charge. It was certainly a desirable accom-
plishment, but the teaching must have been attended with some difficulties.

For the amusememt of my young readers I will
try to describe one of these lessons. Mr. Crawford wished the boys to learn how to enter a
room and pay their respects to the assembled
company.

"Abe, it is your turn," he says.

Abe Lincoln, understanding what is meant,
rose from his seat, and retires from the room.
A moment later a knock is heard at the door.
A scholar, specially deputed to do so—we will

suppose Nat Grigsby—advances to the door and opens it.

Before him stands Abe—tall, awkward, with the lower part of his limbs exposed.

Nat bows, and, taking him by the arm, leads him from bench to bench, presenting him to his fellow-pupils, as though he were a guest going the rounds in a drawing-room. Abe, who was never without a sense of fun, no doubt stole timorous glances askance at his rustic garb as he strode here and there, bowing politely to the boys and girls whom he knew so well. Yet it is possible that this exercise may have made it less awkward for him in later days to attend to his social duties when events brought him prominently before the country.

So far from laughing at Master Crawford's instruction in manners, I am disposed to think very favorably of it. He must on the whole have been a sensible man, and no doubt had a considerable influence over the rough boys who submitted willingly to what possibly struck them as ludicrous.

I doubt, however, with all his pains, whether he succeeded in making Abe Lincoln graceful or courtly. On the whole, he was rather unpromis-

ing material ; being long, lank, and awkward.
Yet this tall, gawky boy was laying the foundation of a noble manhood. He was making the
most of his slender advantages, not dreaming
what greatness the Future had in store for him.

CHAPTER III.

My young readers may naturally feel some curiosity as to the Lincoln family and their previous history.

The grandfather of Abraham was one of the pioneer settlers of Kentucky. About the year 1780 he removed from Rockingham County, Virginia, to what was then an unsettled wilderness. His death was tragical. Four years later, while at work in the field, at some distance from his cabin, he was shot down by a prowling Indian. How his widow managed, with the care of five helpless children, we do not accurately know, but God helps the struggling, and she reared them all till they reached man's and woman's estate. Thomas Lincoln, born in 1778, was the third child, and the future President was his son. He was a good-natured, popular man, but inefficient and un-

(26)

successful, and whatever there was great in his eminent son did not come from him.

Nancy Hanks, Abe's own mother, was born in Virginia, and was probably related to some family emigrating from that State. Dr. Holland says of her : "Mrs. Lincoln, the mother, was evidently a woman out of place among these primitive surroundings. She was five feet five inches high, a slender, pale, sad, and sensitive woman, with much in her nature that was truly heroic, and much that shrank from the rude life around her. A great man never drew his infant life from a purer or more womanly bosom than her own." Though she died young, she had taught her children to read, and so laid the foundation of their education.

When Thomas Lincoln had made up his mind to move from Kentucky, he sold his humble home, or rather bartered it for ten barrels of whisky and twenty dollars in money. It must not be inferred that he was an intemperate man—this would not be true—but money was scarce in those days, and it was common to barter, taking pay in commodities which were marketable. This was before the days of temperance societies ; whisky was generally drunk, even by ministers, and there was little risk in accepting it.

So Thomas Lincoln, leaving home by himself to find a new residence for his family, built a flat-boat, and launched it on the Rolling Fork, a creek emptying into the Ohio River. He reached the river in safety, but then came a disaster. His flat-boat was upset, and two-thirds of his whisky, and many of his housekeeping and farm utensils were lost. He did the best he could, however. With friendly assistance he saved all he was able, and proceeding on his journey, carried his goods about eighteen miles into Spencer County, Indiana, the place where we find him at the commencement of our narrative. He returned to Kentucky for his family, and brought them with him to the new home in the wilderness. Seven days, we are told, were consumed on the journey, though the distance could not have been very great. We can easily imagine what privations and weariness of body this journey involved. People of to-day don't know what "moving" is. They should have lived in in the year 1816, and made a toilsome seven days' march through the wilderness to understand what it meant then.

Nor were their trials and privations over when the moving was accomplished. I am tempted to quote here from Mr. Ward H. Lamon's interesting life of Lincoln, an account of life in the new Indiana home, contained in a letter from Mr. David Turnham, a school-fellow of Abe :

"When my father came here in the Spring of 1819, he settled in Spencer County, within one mile of Thomas Lincoln, then a widower. The chance for schooling was poor ; but, such as it was, Abraham and myself attended the same schools.

"We first had to go seven miles to mill ; and then it was a hand-mill that would grind from ten to fifteen bushels of corn in a day. There was but little wheat grown at that time ; and when we did have wheat, we had to grind it on the mill described, and use it without bolting, as there were no bolts in the country. In the course of two or three years, a man by the name of Huffman built a mill on Anderson River, about twelve miles distant. Abe and I had to do the milling on horseback, frequently going twice to get one grist. Then they began building horse-mills of a little better quality than the hand-mills.

"The country was very rough, especially in the low lands, so thick with brush that a man could scarcely get through on foot. These places were called Roughs. The country abounded in game, such as bears, deer, turkeys, and the smaller game.

"At that time there were a great many deer-licks; and Abe and myself would go to these licks sometimes, and watch of nights to kill deer, though Abe was not so fond of a gun as I was. There were ten or twelve of these licks in a small prairie on the creek, lying be ween Mr. Lincoln's and Mr. Wood's. This gave it the name of Prairie Track of Pigeon Creek."

I have already said that Thomas Lincoln was a carpenter. He did not, however, understand his trade very well, and, though he was employed in small jobs, there is no evidence that he was ever employed to build a house, or was considered competent to do so. In fact, he derived but a small income from his trade,.and probably looked upon himself rather as a farmer than a mechanic. It was a piece of good fortune for himself and his children, that, shiftless and unambitious as he was, he should have won a wife so much more capable and energetic than himself. He was much shorter than his son Abe, being an inch or two under six feet. In some respects they were alike, however, for Thomas Lincoln had a gift for telling stories, and would sit about at " stores," or under trees, and amuse his neighbors with an inexhaustible fund of anecdotes. Of education he had little or none. He could write his name, having learned this much from his first wife, Abe's mother, but he never had the ambition or perseverance to go farther up the hill of learning. We are told, however, that he was in favor of his children's obtaining an education, though it was probably the mother and step-mother to whom Abe and his sister were especially indebted for such advantages as they enjoyed. I may say, however, that the most valuable part of Abraham Lincoln's education was not derived from books. He was a close and keen observer of men and things, and few men excelled him in insight into human nature, and the motives, the weaknesses, and the subterfuges of men. Yet with all this knowledge of the bad as well as the good that was in men, he was always a kindly and sympathetic judge and critic.

I suppose all boys at some time or other in their

early years have a narrow escape. My young readers may be interested to know how near we came to losing our future President. It was when Abe was seven years old, and before he removed to Indiana.

He was accustomed to go on numerous tramps with his cousin, Dennis Hanks, who sought to initiate him into the mysteries of fishing. On one occasion he attempted to " coon " across Knot Creek, by swinging over on a sycamore tree. But he lost his hold and tumbled into the deep water. He would have drowned but for the exertions of his boy companion, who had great difficulty in saving him. The readers of Garfield's Life will remember how he also came near death by drowning, when considerably older than Abe was at this juncture. But God looks after the lives of His chosen instruments, and saves them for His work.

There is no doubt that Abe found plenty to do outside of school. In fact, that did not take up much of his time, for we are told that, adding together all the time he spent in attendance, the aggregate would not exceed a year.

As to the sort of work he did, his father found work for him on the land which he had under cultivation. Then the "chores" which boys in such households are always called upon to do, in his case exacted more time on account of the lack of average accommodations. For instance, the water had to be brought from a spring a mile away, and Abe and his sister were employed to fetch it. There was no water to be had nearer, except what was collected in holes in the ground after a rain, and this was necessarily unfit for drinking, or, indeed, any other purpose unless strained. But Abe is not to be pitied for the hardships of his lot. That is the way strong men are made.

CHAPTER IV.

ABE'S SCHOOLING.

"SPELL *defied!*"

This question was put a class in spelling by the master.

The first pupil in the straggling line of backwoods boys and girls who stood up in class, answered with some hesitation: "D-e-f-i-d-e, defied."

The master frowned.

"Next!" he called sharply.

The next improved upon the effort of the first speller, and in a confident tone answered.

"D-e-f-y-d-e."

"Wrong again! The next may try it," said the teacher.

"D-e-f-y-d!" said the third scholar.

"Worse and worse! You are entitled to a medal!" said Crawford, sarcastically. "Next!"

"D-e-f-y-e-d!" was the next attempt.

"Really, you do me great credit," said the teacher, a frown gathering on his brow. "You can't spell an easy word of two syllables. It is shameful. I'll keep the whole class in all the rest of the day, if necessary, till the word is spelled correctly."

It now became the turn of a young girl named Roby, who was a favorite with Abe. She was a pretty girl, but, nevertheless, the terrible word puzzled her. In her perplexity she chanced to turn toward the seat at the window occupied by her long-legged friend, Abe.

Abe was perhaps the best speller in school. A word like defied was easy enough to him, and he wanted to help the girl through.

As Miss Roby looked at him she saw a smile upon his face, as he significantly touched his *eye* with his finger. The girl took the hint, and spelled the word correctly.

"Right at last!" said Master Crawford, whose back was turned, and who had not seen Abe's dumb show. "It's lucky for you all that one of the class knew how to spell, or I would have kept my word, and kept you all in."

Though Master Crawford's school had a de-

partment of manners, there was no department
of English composition. Abe took this up on
his own account, according to his schoolmate,
Nat Grigsby, and probably the teacher consented
to examine his essays, though he did not require
them of his other pupils. Considering the kindness of heart which he afterward exhibited on many
occasions, my readers will not be surprised to hear
that his first composition was against cruelty to
animals. This is said to have been called forth
oy the conduct of some of his fellow-pupils in
catching terrapins and putting coals of fire on
their backs.

After a time Master Crawford's school was discontinued, and some two or three years later Abe
attended another, kept by a Mr. Swaney. It gives
us an idea of the boy's earnest desire to obtain an
education, when we learn that he had to walk
four and a half miles to it from his father's house,
and this walk had to be repeated, of course, in
the afternoon. How many of my young readers
would care sufficiently for an education to walk
nine miles a day, to and from school?

We are told that the new school-house was no
more impressive, architecturally, than the first, al-

ready described. In fact, it was very similar, though it had two chimneys instead of one. The course of instruction does not seem to have been any higher than at Mr. Crawford's school. The department of "manners" was omitted, though it is doubtful whether many of the pupils could have appeared to advantage in a city ball-room.

Probably Abe did not attend Mr. Swaney's school many weeks, and this, we are told, was the end of his school attendance anywhere. He had, however, in that short time imbibed a love of learning, which is to be credited rather to his own tastes than to the influence of his teachers, and carried on by himself the studies of which he had learned something in the humble back-woods school. We are told that he was already the equal of his teachers in learning, which probably was not saying much. Nevertheless he did not regard his education as finished. He had his books, and kept on studying at home, or wherever he was employed. In the hard work which fell to his lot he did not take much interest. He knew that it was necessary, but he did not enjoy it. He preferred to labor with his brain rather than with his hands, and often seemed so listless and preoccupied that he got the reputation of being " awful lazy."

This is what his neighbor, Romine, says of him : " He worked for me; was always reading and thinking; used to get mad at him. I say, Abe was awful lazy; he would laugh, and talk, and crack jokes and tell stories all the time; didn't love work, but did dearly love his pay. He worked for me frequently, a few days only at a time. . . . . Lincoln said to me one day, that his father taught him to work, but never learned him to love it."

All the information we can obtain about this early time is interesting, for it was then that Abe was laying the foundation of his future eminence. His mind and character were slowly developing, and shaping themselves for the future.

From Mr. Lamon's Life I quote a paragraph which will throw light upon his habits and tastes at the age of seventeen :

" Abe loved to lie under a shade-tree, or up in the loft of the cabin, and read, cipher, and scribble. At night he sat by the chimney 'jamb,' and ciphered by the light of the fire, on the wooden fire-shovel. When the shovel was fairly covered, he would shave it off with Tom Lincoln's drawing-knife, and begin again. In the day-time he used boards for the same purpose, out of doors, and went through the shaving process everlastingly. His step-mother repeats often that 'he read every book he could lay his hands on.' She says, 'Abe read diligently. He read every book he could lay his hands on, and when he came across a passage that struck him, he would write it down on boards if he had no paper, and keep it there until he did get paper. Then he would rewrite it, look at it, repeat it. He had a copy-book, a kind of scrap-book, in which he put down all things, and thus preserved them.' "

I am tempted also to quote a reminiscence of John Hanks, who lived with the Lincolns from the time Abe was fourteen to the time he became eighteen years of age : " When Lincoln—Abe— and I returned to the house from work, he would go to the cupboard, snatch a piece of corn-bread, take down a book, sit down on a chair, cock his legs up as high as his head, and read. He and I worked barefooted, grubbed it, ploughed, mowed, and cradled together ; ploughed corn, gathered it, and shucked corn. Abraham read constantly when he had opportunity."

It may well be supposed, however, that the
books upon which Abe could lay hands were few
in number. There were no libraries, either public or private, in the neighborhood, and he was
obliged to read what he could get rather than
those which he would have chosen, had he been
able to select from a large collection. Still, it is
a matter of interest to know what books he actu-
ally did read at this formative period. Some of
them certainly were worth reading, such as
"Æsop's Fables," "Robinson Crusoe," "Pil-
grim's Progress," a History of the United States,
and Weem's "Life of Washington." The last
book Abe borrowed from a neighbor, old Josiah
Crawford, (I follow the statement of Mr. Lamon,
rather than of Dr. Holland, who says it was Master Crawford, his teacher). When not reading it,
he laid it away in a part of the cabin where he
thought it would be free from harm, but it so
happened that just behind the shelf on which he
placed it was a great crack between the logs of
the wall. One night a storm came up suddenly,
the rain beat in through the crevice, and soaked
the borrowed book through and through. The
book was almost utterly spoiled. Abe felt very

uneasy, for a book was valuable in his eyes, as well as in the eyes of its owner.

He took the damaged volume and trudged over to Mr. Crawford's in some perplexity and mortification.

"Well, Abe, what brings you over so early?" said Mr. Crawford.

"I've got some bad news for you," answered Abe, with lengthened face.

"Bad news! What is it?"

"You know the book you lent me—the 'Life of Washington'?"

"Yes, yes."

"Well, the rain last night spoiled it," and Abe showed the book, wet to a pulp inside, at the same time explaining how it had been injured.

"It's too bad, I vum! You'd ought to pay for it, Abe. You must have been dreadful careless!"

"I'd pay for it if I had any money, Mr. Crawford."

"If you've got no money, you can work it out," said Crawford.

"I'll do whatever you think right."

So it was arranged that Abe should work three days for Crawford, "pulling fodder," the value of his labor being rated at twenty-five cents a day. As the book had cost seventy-five cents this would be regarded as satisfactory. So Abe worked his three days, and discharged the debt. Mr. Lamon is disposed to find fault with Crawford for exacting this penalty, but it appears to me only equitable, and I am glad to think that Abe was willing to act honorably in the matter.

CHAPTER V.

IF Abe's knowledge had increased in proportion to the increase in his stature, he would have been unusually learned at the age of seventeen, for he stood at that time nearly six feet four inches in his stockings, and, boy as he was, was taller than any man in the vicinity.

I must not omit to state that he had a remarkable memory, and this was of great service to him in his early efforts at oratory. Mr. Lamon tells us that

"He frequently amused his young companions by repeating to them long passages from the books he had been reading. On Monday mornings he would mount a stump and deliver, with a wonderful approach to exactness, the sermon he had heard the day before. His taste for public speaking appeared to be natural and irresistible."

(43)

Let me describe one of the scenes in which Abe often took part.

Mr. and Mrs. Lincoln have gone to church, for it is Sunday morning. The children are excused on account of the distance, and are left at home to fill up the time as they may.

"Come in," said Abe, appearing at the door of the cabin, " I'm going to preach."

With more willingness, perhaps, than if the services were to be conducted by a grown-up minister, the other young people in the family enter and sit down in decorous style, while Abe pulls down the Bible, reads a passage, and gives out a hymn. This is sung with more earnestness than musical taste, and then the young preacher begins his sermon.

I am sure we should all like to have been present, and should have listened with interest while the gaunt, awkward boy, gesticulating with his long arms, delivered a homily not original with himself, but no doubt marked by some of his peculiarities.

We are told that this young audience, the girls probably, were sometimes affected to tears. One might have been tempted to predict that the boy would develop into a preacher when he grew to man's estate. But Abe did not confine himself to "preaching." He was just as fond of other kinds of public speaking. Sometimes in the harvest field he mounted a stump and began to talk on political subjects.

More than once Thomas Lincoln, going out to the field, found work at a standstill, and a little group collected at one point, Abe being the central figure.

"What's all this?" he would ask angrily.

"It's Abe," one of the hands would answer. "He's givin' us a rousin' speech on politics."

"I'll rouse him!" said the incensed father. "Only let me get at him!"

So he would push his way into the crowd unseen by Abe, and would suddenly seize his son by the collar and drag him from his extemporized rostrum.

"Now go to work!" he would exclaim in irritation. "You can't make your living by talking."

Abe, with a comical smile, would close his speech, to resume it on some more auspicious occasion.

I have already said that Thomas Lincoln was a carpenter, though a poor one. Abe sometimes worked with him in the shop, but had no idea of learning the trade. He preferred to work in the field, and, as he could not fill up his time on the four acres his father cultivated, he hired out to any one of the neighbors who required his services.

No prediction could have surprised his employers more than that the tall, awkward youth, who had grown out of his clothes, would hereafter hold in his hands the destinies of the country, and guide it triumphantly to the end of a protracted and bloody struggle.

The career of Lincoln is a striking illustration of the often-repeated saying that " Truth is stranger than fiction."

While there is room for suspicion that Abe was not fond of physical labor, he is said to have worked very satisfactorily for those who employed him. He had no troublesome pride, but was willing to do anything that was asked, and pleased the women especially by never objecting when called upon " to make a fire, carry water. or nurse a baby."

I am tempted to quote from Mr. Lamon's interesting volume an account furnished him by Mrs. Elizabeth Crawford of the people among whom Abe lived and some of their peculiarities. It throws light upon the homely side of the future President's character and speech:

"You wish me to tell you how the people used to go to meeting—how far they went. At that time we thought it nothing to go eight or ten miles. The old ladies did not stop for the want of a shawl, or cloak, or riding-dress, or two horses in the winter-time; but they would put on their husbands' old overcoats, and wrap up their little ones, and take one or two of them on their beasts, and their husbands would walk, and they would go to church, and stay in the neighborhood until the next day, and then go home. The old men would start out of their fields from their work, or out of the woods from hunting, with their guns on their shoulders, and go to church. Some of them dressed in deer-skin pants and moccasins, hunting-shirts, with a rope or leather strap around them. They would come in laughing, shake hands all around, sit down and talk about the game they had killed, or some

other work they had done, and smoke their pipes
together with the old ladies. If in warm weather,
they would kindle up a little fire out in the meeting-house yard to light their pipes.

"If in winter-time, they would hold church in
some of the neighbors' houses. At such times
they were always treated with the utmost of kindness; a bottle of whisky, a pitcher of water, su-
gar, and glass were set out, or a basket of apples
or turnips, or some pies and cakes. Apples were
scarce them times. Sometimes potatoes were
used for a treat. (I must tell you that the first
treat I ever received in old Mr. Linkhern's house
—that was our President's father's house—was a
plate of potatoes, washed and pared very nicely,
and handed 'round. It was something new to
me, for I had never seen a raw potato eaten before. I looked to see how they made use of
them. They took off a potato, and ate them like
apples).

"Thus they spent the time till time for preaching to commence, then they would all take their
seats; the preacher would take his stand, draw
his coat, open his shirt-collar, and commence
service by singing and prayer; take his text and

preach till the sweat would roll off in great drops. Shaking hands and singing then ended the service. The people seemed to enjoy religion more in them days than they do now. They were glad to see each other, and enjoyed themselves better than they do now."

Such is the testimony of an old lady, who, like old people generally, is prone to praise the past at the expense of the present.

The ladies in Abe's early days wore "corn-field bonnets, scoop-shaped, flaring in front, and long, though narrow behind." They were as fond of dancing as our city ladies, but did not find an elaborate toilet so essential. It was not uncommon for both sexes to discard shoes and dance barefooted. I have no doubt they enjoyed themselves as well, if not better, in this absence of restraint, than their more polished sisters who are to be found in city drawing-rooms to-day.

Brought up in such an unconventional atmosphere, it is not surprising that Abraham Lincoln never set much value upon form and ceremony, and sometimes shocked his more conventional political associates.

Mr. John B. Alley, a member of the Massachusetts Congressional delegation during the war of the Rebellion, described to me on one occasion how much shocked Senator Sumner was when, on calling upon the President, in company with Lord Lyons, the English Minister, they found him sitting at ease in true Western style, with his heels resting on the table.

"How are you, Sumner?" was the President's greeting. "Take a seat, Lord Lyons."

And all the while the good President did not seem to be aware that he was acting in a manner unbecoming the dignity of a great ruler. Yet he might have been aware of it, and secretly enjoyed the annoyance of his distinguished guests. I am not prepared to recommend my young readers to imitate Lincoln in this respect, but I wish them to understand how he was affected by his early acquaintances and surroundings. We shall all agree that there are many things more important than polished manners and personal dignity, and we shall find hereafter that Abraham Lincoln, in spite of his homely manners, was a Providential man, who served his country in her hour of need, as probably no other could have done.

CHAPTER VI.

A RIVER TRIP.

THUS passed the early years of Abraham Li. coln. He was approaching manhood, well prepared physically to undertake its responsibilities, but with a very slender stock of knowledge. He had, however, acquired a taste for learning, and was a close, careful, and shrewd observer. He had also the ability to speak fluently in rough-and-ready style on any subject of which he knew anything. Of the world he had seen very little, but his knowledge in that direction was to be extended by a trip down the Ohio and Mississippi Rivers, which he took at the age of nineteen.

Early in 1828 he chanced to be in the employ of Mr. Gentry, the founder of Gentryville, a village which had sprung up since Thomas Lincoln had lived in the neighborhood.

One morning Allen Gentry said to Lincoln:

"Abe, how would you like to go to New Orleans with me?"

"Are you going?" asked Abe eagerly.

"Yes, I am almost sure of going. I have spoken to father about letting me go on a trading trip down the river, and I should like to have you go with me."

"I'll go," said Abe promptly, "if you'll give me the chance."

"There is no one I would like better to have with me," answered Allen, "and I can't go alone."

He had good reason for preferring Abe to any of his other friends, not only that young Lincoln was very strong and capable, but because he had then, as in after years, a pleasant humor, which showed itself in stories which he had pat for any occasion. Though homely enough, they were never destitute of point, and were brimming over with shrewd fun.

To a backwoods boy the proposed trip was as fascinating—perhaps more so, notwithstanding the hard work involved—as a European trip nowadays. There was constant variety; there was a varying panorama of meadows and villages, as they floated down the rapid current to the mouth of the great river.

Mr. Gentry favored his son's plan, and preparations were speedily made.

The craft on which the two young men embarked was à flat-boat, roughly made. It was loaded with a cargo of bacon and other produce, such as it was thought would sell readily down South. Abe was the leader of the expedition, and the business was under his care, inexperienced as he was. He was ready to take the responsibility then as in after years, when he piloted the ship of State with its valuable cargo over rougher waters.

My young readers may be interested to know that he was paid eight dollars per month, eating and sleeping on board, and that he was furnished with free return passage on a steamboat.

The custom was to stop at all important points and seek an opportunity to trade. During the night the boat was tied up to the shore, and the two young men slept on board in the little cabin.

Generally, there was no risk of robbery or hostile attack; but one night, a few miles below

Baton Rouge, the two young men were startled by hearing footsteps on board.

"What's that?" inquired Allen, starting.

"We must have visitors," replied Abe quietly.

"Then they are not the right kind. They must be thieves."

"I reckon so. Let us get up and give them a reception."

Rising as quietly as possible, Abe and Allen Gentry looked out and saw that the invading force consisted of seven stalwart negroes. They were of the same class, only bolder, as the chicken thieves, who visit their neighbors' hen-roosts.

"They are after our bacon," said Abe. "We must try to save our bacon if we can," he added, with a humorous smile.

Now, it requires some courage to get up in the dead of night and confront a gang of thieves, especially when they are seven to two, but the two young men were courageous, and they had no idea of submitting tamely to robbery.

"Bring the guns, Abe!" exclaimed Allen in a loud tone, intending to be heard by the marauders. "Bring the guns; shoot them!"

Lincoln had no gun, but he had a huge bludg-

eon, and he sprang upon them, belaboring them
with all the strength of his sinewy arm. No won
der they were terrified as they surveyed the commanding stature of the stripling and felt his terrible blows. Seven to two as they were, they
found discretion the better part of valor, and fled,
some jumping into the water.

But Allen and Abe were not satisfied with this
victory. They felt that they must give their guilty
visitors a lesson. So they chased them far back into
the country, and, on returning, thought it best to
cut loose and float down the river, lest they should
have another call from their unwelcome visitors,
possibly reinforced by others of the same stripe.
These seven negroes little dreamed that the intrepid young man who so belabored them was destined under the providence of God to be the champion and deliverer of their race from the bondage
under which they groaned. I may add that Abe
himself would perhaps have been even more surprised could this have been revealed to him, as,
bludgeon in hand, he chased the flying negroes
over the meadows.

The time consumed in this river trip was about
three months. The result was satisfactory to his

employer, and showed that his confidence in his young neighbor was not misplaced. On his return, young Lincoln worked as before, wherever opportunity offered, and probably, being under age, turned in his earnings to the common fund. But the time was coming when the family were to find a new home. Born in Kentucky, Abe had spent rather more than half his life in Indiana, but a new State—the one which now claims him as her most distinguished son—was soon to receive him. In the spring of 1830, Thomas Lincoln pulled up stakes and moved to Illinois. But his immediate family was smaller now than when he left Kentucky. Abe's sister had married early, and survived her marriage but about a year. However, there were the step-children, and the families of Dennis Hanks and Levi Hall, so that the company numbered thirteen in all. Fifteen days' journey brought them to a point ten miles west of Decatur, where a small house was erected on the north bank of the north fork of the Sangamon River. Abe and his cousin John broke up fifteen acres of land and split rails enough to serve as a fence. This was the first time, so far as we know, that young Lincoln justified the appellation, which clung to him in after years, of *rail-splitter*.

But young Lincoln was now nearing the age of twenty-one. Largely because of his affection for his step-mother, to whom he was always ready to acknowledge his obligations, he had remained about home much longer than many sons, who forget filial duty under the impulse of ambition or enterprise. So his twenty-first birthday found him still a member of the home household. Then, naturally enough, he felt that it was time to set up for himself. So in March or April he left home, but he seemed to have formed no definite plans—none at least likely to carry him far away from home. He was a candidate for labor, and took whatever offered, but the proceeds went into his own pocket.

One of the "jobs" which he undertook was splitting rails for a man named Kirkpatrick. I quote from Dr. Holland in reference to this period:

"A man who used to work with Abraham occasionally during his first year in Illinois, says that at that time he was the roughest-looking person he ever saw. He was tall, angular, and ungainly, and wore trousers made of flax and tow, cut tight at the ankle, and out at both knees. He was known to be very poor, but he was a welcome guest in every house in the neighborhood. This informant speaks of splitting rails with Abraham, and reveals some interesting facts concerning wages. Money was a commodity never reckoned upon. Abraham split rails to get clothing, and he made a bargain with Mrs. Nancy Miller to split four hundred rails for every yard of brown jeans, dyed with white walnut bark, that would be necessary to make him a pair of trousers. In those days he used to walk four, six, and seven miles to his work."

My young readers will be interested in a story which relates to this time. Abe was working for a Mr. Brown, "raising a crap," when a traveler stopped at the house and inquired if he could obtain accommodations for the night, there being no tavern near.

"Well," said Mr. Brown, "we can feed your crittur and give you somethin' to eat, but we can't lodge you unless you can sleep on the same bed with the hired man."

The man, who was sprucely dressed, hesitated, and inquired:

"Who is he?"

"Well," said Mr. Brown, "you can come and see him."

So the man followed the farmer to the back of the house, where young Lincoln lay extended at full length on the ground in the shade.

"There he is," said Brown.

"Well, I think he'll do," said the stranger, and he stayed and slept with Abe, whom he then no doubt looked down upon as his " social" inferior. Could he have looked forward with prophetic ken, he would have felt honored by such chance association with a man destined to be President of the United States.

I am sorry that some doubts are thrown upon this story, but I have ventured to tell it, for the vivid contrast between the position which young Lincoln undoubtedly occupied at that time and that which in after years he so adequately filled.

CHAPTER VII.

LINCOLN AS A CLERK

YOUNG Lincoln's successful trip to New Orleans led to his engagement for a similar trip in the early part of 1831. With him were associated John Hanks and John Johnston. Their employer was a Mr. Denton Offutt, of Lexington, Kentucky, and a part of the cargo consisted of a drove of hogs. Each of the three was to be paid at the rate of fifty cents per day, and the round sum of sixty dollars divided between them. Abe considered this very good pay, and was very glad to make the engagement. The three young men not only managed the boat, but built it, and this retarded the expedition. We read with some interest that while they were boarding themselves at Sangamontown, while building the boat, Abe officiated as cook to the entire satisfaction of his associates.

"At New Orleans," says John Hanks, "we saw negroes chained, maltreated, whipped, and scourged. Lincoln saw it; his heart bled, he said nothing much, was silent from feeling, was sad, looked bad, felt bad, was thoughtful and abstracted. I can say, knowing it, that it was on this trip that he formed his opinions of slavery. It run its iron in him then and there,—May, 1831. I have heard him say so often and often."

One day, soon after his return from his second river trip, Abe received a visit from a muscular, powerfully-built man, who accosted him thus: "You are Abe Lincoln, I reckon?"

"Yes," said Abe; "you are right there."

"I've heard you can wrestle some," continued the stranger.

"A little," answered young Lincoln, modestly.

"I've come to wrestle with you to see who's the best man. My name's Daniel Needham."

The stranger announced his name with evident pride, and young Lincoln recognized it as that of a man who had a high reputation as an amateur pugilist.

"I'm glad to know you," said Lincoln, "and I don't mind accepting your challenge."

Abe valued his popularity among the boys, and, though he did not feel sure of the result, he felt that it would not do to back out.   He would lose his reputation, which was considerable.

"Where shall it be?" asked Needham.

"Just where and when you like," answered Abe, promptly.

So the meeting was fixed in the "greenwood" at Wabash Point, and there it was that the two met in friendly rivalry.

Though Daniel Needham was older and more firmly knit, Lincoln was sinewy and strong, and his superior height, and long arms and legs gave him a great advantage—sufficient to compensate for his youth and spareness.

The result was that Abe achieved victory in short order.   He threw his older opponent twice with so much ease that Needham rose to his feet very much mortified as well as astonished.

"Lincoln," said he, making the confession reluctantly, "you have thrown me twice, but you can't whip me."

"Are you satisfied that I can throw you?" asked Abe.   "If you are not, and must be convinced through a thrashing, I will do that too for your sake."

"I reckon we'll put it off," said Needham, finding his young rival more willing than he had expected. He had hoped that, though not shrinking from a friendly wrestling contest, Abe might hesitate to meet him in a more serious encounter.

I have told this story partly because I know my young readers would be interested in it, partly to give an idea of the strength and athletic power of the hero of my story.

But wrestling contests would not earn a living for young Lincoln. He was in search of employment, and found it. As one thing leads to another, the same man who had sent him to New Orleans in charge of a flat-boat, opened a store at New Salem, and needing a clerk, bethought himself of young Lincoln. Abe unpacked the goods upon their arrival, and worked energetically to put them in order. With a new store-book, serving as a ledger, and a pen behind his ear, he made his début as a "first clerk" of the leading mercantile establishment in the town. In the readiness with which he turned from one thing to another, Abe might well be taken for a typical Yankee, though born in Kentucky.

We are now to look upon the future President

in a new capacity. As a clerk he proved honest and efficient, and my readers will be interested in some illustrations of the former trait which I find in Dr. Holland's interesting volume.

One day a woman came into the store and purchased sundry articles. They footed up two dollars and six and a quarter cents, or the young clerk thought they did. We do not hear nowadays of six and a quarter cents, but this was a coin borrowed from the Spanish currency, and was well known in my own boyhood.

The bill was paid, and the woman was entirely satisfied. But the young store-keeper, not feeling quite sure as to the accuracy of his calculation, added up the items once more. To his dismay he found that the sum total should have been but two dollars.

"I've made her pay six and a quarter cents too much," said Abe, disturbed.

It was a trifle, and many clerks would have dismissed it as such. But Abe was too conscientious for that.

"The money must be paid back," he decided.

This would have been easy enough had the woman lived "just round the corner," but, as the young man knew, she lived between two and three miles away. This, however, did not alter the matter. It was night, but he closed and locked the store, and walked to the residence of his customer. Arrived there, he explained the matter, paid over the six and a quarter cents, and returned satisfied. If I were a capitalist, I would be willing to lend money to such a young man without security.

Here is another illustration of young Lincoln's strict honesty :

A woman entered the store and asked for half a pound of tea.

The young clerk weighed it out, and handed it to her in a parcel. This was the last sale of the day.

The next morning, when commencing his duties, Abe discovered a four-ounce weight on the scales. It flashed upon him at once that he had used this in the sale of the night previous, and so, of course, given his customer short weight. I am afraid that there are many country merchants who would not have been much worried by this discovery. Not so the young clerk in whom we are interested. He weighed out the balance of the half pound, shut up store, and carried it to the defrauded customer. I think my young readers will begin to see that the name so often given, in later times, to President Lincoln, of "Honest Old Abe," was well deserved. A man who begins by strict honesty in his youth is not likely to change as he grows older, and mercantile honesty is some guarantee of political honesty.

There is another incident for which I am also indebted to Dr. Holland:

The young clerk was waiting upon two or three ladies, when a noted bully entered the store, and began to talk in a manner offensive not only to the ladies, but to any person of refinement.

Young Lincoln leaned over the counter, and said quietly, "Don't you see that ladies are present?"

"What is that to me?" demanded the bully.

"Out of respect for them, will you stop your rough talk?"

"I will talk as I please, and I should like to see the man that will stop me," answered the bully, arrogantly. "If you think you are the better man, we'll try it on the spot."

Lincoln began to see that the man meant to

force a quarrel upon him, and he did not shrink from it.

"If you will wait till the ladies retire," he said quietly, "I will give you any satisfaction you wish."

The ladies had by this time completed their purchases, and were glad to leave the store.

No sooner had they left than the bully broke out into a storm of abuses and insults. The young clerk listened with the quiet patience habitual to him, and finally observed: "Well, if you must be whipped, I suppose I may as well whip you as any other man."

"That's what I'm after," answered the bully.

"Come outdoors, then," said Lincoln.

Abe, when they were fairly outside, thought there was no need of further delay. He grappled with the bully, threw him upon the ground with ease, and, holding him there, rubbed some "smart-weed" in his face and eyes till he bellowed for mercy.

"Do you give up?" asked Abe, in no way excited.

"Yes, yes!"

Upon this, Lincoln went for some water, washed his victim's face, and did what he could to alleviate his sufferings. It is safe to say that the fellow never wanted another dose of the same medicine. It will further interest my young readers to learn that, so far from feeling a grudge against Lincoln, the bully became his fast friend, and behaved henceforth in a more creditable manner.

CHAPTER VIII.

THOUGH the young clerk proved faithful and efficient, his whole time was not taken up by his duties in Offutt's store. Knowing well the defects of his education, it occurred to him that he could use profitably some of his leisure by employing it in study. He knew little or nothing of English grammar, and this was likely to interfere with him if called upon to act in any public capacity where he would be required to make speeches.

"I have a notion to study English grammar," he said to Mr. Graham, the schoolmaster.

"That is the best thing you can do, if you expect to enter political life," said the teacher in reply.

"Where do you think I can find a grammar?" asked Lincoln.

It must be remembered that educational books, and indeed books of any kind, were scarce in those days.

"I think you will find one at Vaner's."

"I will go at once and see," said Lincoln.

He set out at once, though Vaner's was six miles distant, but such a walk did not trouble the young man at all. I am sure it will strike some of my young readers who dislike grammar, as odd that he should be willing to take so long a walk with such an object in view; but they too might do the same if they were as earnestly bent upon self-improvement as our hero. It is enough to say that he succeeded in obtaining the coveted book, and began at once to study it. Sometimes he was able to go out of doors and lie under a shade-tree: at other times he stretched his long, ungainly form on the counter and pored intently over the little book. I don't know whether the obscure little text-book is still in existence; if it were, it would be a valuable memorial of this transition period in the young man's mental growth.

The time came for a change in young Lincoln's mode of life. Mr. Offutt's business declined, and the store was closed. He was once more out of employment. Now it happened about this time that the peace of this region was disturbed by a series of Indian difficulties. Black Hawk, a chief of the Sacs, was the instigator and Indian leader. He was a man of commanding presence and superior abilities. In defiance of a warning given him by General Atkinson, commanding the United States troops at Rock Island, he left his reservation, and announced his intention of ascending the Rock River to the territory of the Winnebagoes. The force under General Atkinson being small, he issued a call for volunteers. One company was raised in New Salem and the vicinity, and Lincoln enlisted. Though without military experience, he was elected to the post of Captain by a large majority of the company, and accepted. This was a tribute to his popularity among his friends and neighbors.

Though the Black Hawk campaign was in no way remarkable, and involved very little fighting, it is noteworthy, as Dr. Holland remarks, that two men afterward Presidents of the United States were engaged in it. These were Zachary Taylor and Abraham Lincoln. I do not propose to enter into a detailed account of this campaign and of Lincoln's part in it; I prefer to quote Mr. Lincoln's own account of it, years afterward, when a member of the House of Representatives at Washington. It was during the political campaign when General Cass was the Democratic candidate, and was intended to ridicule the claims of his friends, that he had rendered distinguished military service to the republic.

"By the way, Mr. Speaker," said Mr. Lincoln, "do you know I am a military hero? Yes, sir, in the days of the Black Hawk war, I fought, bled, and came away. Speaking of General Cass' career reminds me of my own. I was not at Sillman's Defeat, but I was about as near it as Cass to Hull's surrender; and, like him, I saw the place soon afterward. It is quite certain I did not break my sword, for I had none to break; but I bent my musket pretty badly on one occasion. If General Cass went in advance of me in picking whortleberries, I guess I surpassed him in charges upon the wild onions. If he saw any live, fighting Indian, it was more than I did; but I had a good many bloody struggles with the mosquitoes, and although I never fainted from loss of blood, I can tru.y say I was often very hungry."

When Mr. Lincoln himself became a candidate for the Presidency, an attempt was made to make capital for him out of this military episode, but fortunately he possessed more substantial claims than this.

Though there was little fighting to be done, there was an occasion that tested the young Captain's courage and resolution. As the incident is characteristic of Lincoln, and shows his love of justice and humanity, I will transcribe, as better than any paraphrase of my own, the account given by Mr. Lamon in his Life of Lincoln :

" One day, during these many marches and counter-marches, an old Indian found his way into the camp, weary, hungry, and helpless. He professed to be a friend of the whites; and, although it was an exceedingly perilous experiment for one of his color, he ventured to throw himself upon the mercy of the soldiers. But the men first murmured, and then broke out into fierce cries for his blood.

" 'We have come out to fight the Indians,' said they, 'and by G— we intend to do it!'

" The poor Indian, now in the extremity of his distress and trouble, did what he ought to have done before: he threw down before his assailants a soiled and crumpled paper which he implored them to read before his life was taken. It was a letter of character and safe conduct from Gen. Cass, pronouncing him a faithful man, who had done good service in the cause for which this army was enlisted. But it was too late; the men refused to read it, or thought it a forgery, and were rushing with fury upon the defenceless old savage, when Capt. Lincoln bounded between them and their appointed victim.

" ' Men,' said he, and his voice for a moment stilled the agitation around him, ' *this must not be done; he must not be shot and killed by us.*"

" ' But,' said some of them, ' the Indian is a spy.'

" Lincoln knew that his own life was now in only less danger than that of the poor creature that cowered behind him. During the whole of this scene Capt. Lincoln seemed to rise to an unusual height of stature. The towering form, the passion and resolution in his face, the physical power and terrible will exhibited in every motion of his body, every gesture of his arm, produced an effect upon the furious mob as unexpected perhaps to him as to any one else. They paused, listened, fell back, and then sullenly obeyed what seemed to be the voice of reason as well as authority. But there were still some murmurs of disappointed rage and half-suppressed exclamations, which looked toward vengeance of some kind At length one of the men, a little bolder than the rest, but evidently feeling that he spoke for the whole, cried out:

" ' This is cowardly on your part, Lincoln ! '

" Whereupon the tall Captain's figure stretched a few inches higher again. He looked down upon these varlets who would have murdered a defenceless old Indian and now quailed before his single hand, with lofty contempt. The oldest of his acquaintances, even Bill Green, who saw him grapple Jack Armstrong and defy the bullies at his back, never saw him so much aroused before.

" ' If any man thinks I am a coward, let him test it,' said he.

" ' Lincoln,' responded a new voice, ' you are stronger and heavier than we are.'

"'This you can guard against; choose your weapons,' returned the rigid Captain.

"Whatever may be said of Mr. Lincoln's choice of means for the preservation of military discipline, it was certainly very effectual in this case. There was no more disaffection in his camp, and the word 'coward' was never coupled with his name again. Mr. Lincoln understood his men better than those who would be disposed to criticise his conduct. He has often declared himself that his life and character were both at stake, and would probably have been lost had he not at that supremely critical moment forgotten the officer and asserted the man To have ordered the offenders under arrest would have created a powerful mutiny; to have tried and punished them would have been impossible. They could scarcely be called soldiers; they were merely armed citizens, with a nominal military organization. They were but recently enlisted, and their term of service was about to expire. Had he preferred charges against them, and offered to submit their differences to a court of any sort, it would have been regarded as an act of personal pusillanimity, and his efficiency would have been gone forever."

Then, as afterward, Lincoln proved to be the man for the emergency. This humble captain of volunteers was selected by Providence to guide and direct his countrymen in the greatest and most bloody civil contest that was ever waged, and at all times of doubt, danger, and perplexity he manifested the same calm courage, the same firm resolution, and the same humanity, which made him at the age of twenty-three the intrepid champion of a friendless old Indian.

CHAPTER IX.

IN THE LEGISLATURE.

My young readers will have noticed how extremely slender thus far had been the educational advantages of young Lincoln. Of the thousands of men who have risen to eminence in this country from similar poverty, few have had so little to help them. In England the path of promotion is more difficult, and I doubt whether any one circumstanced as Abraham Lincoln was could ever have reached a commanding position. It will be interesting in this connection to read the statement made by John Bright at his recent installation as Lord Rector of Glasgow University. It will show what a difference there is between limited advantages in England and in America:

"I am an entire stranger to University life in the University sense," says Mr. Bright. "I may be said to be a man who never had the advantages of education. I had the teaching of some French—as Englishmen teach French, and I had the advantages of a year's instruction in Latin by a most admirable tutor—a countryman of yours from the University of Edinburgh. But there was not much Greek—not so much that any trace of it is left. There was nothing in the shape of mathematics or science. Looking at education as you take it, I am a person who had the misfortune to have had almost none of it in my youth. You will not, therefore, be surprised if I feel a certain humiliation in seeming to teach you anything, and if I feel a strong sense of envy —but not a blamable envy—that I never possessed the advantages which are placed within your reach. But if I had no education such as colleges and universities give, if my school-life ended at the precise time when your university career begins; if I am unknown to literature and to science and to arts, I ask myself what is it that has brought me within the range of your sympathies—brought me to this distinguished position? I suppose it must be because you have some sympathy with my labors. You believe that I have been in some sort a political teacher; that I have

taken some pains and perhaps have been of some
service in the legislation and government of our
country."

Had Lincoln possessed one-half the educational
equipment of John Bright when he entered upon
political life he would have felt much better satisfied.

Abraham Lincoln on his return from the
Black Hawk campaign was twenty-three years
old. Though he was about as poor as he had
always been, he was rich in the good opinion of
his friends and neighbors. This is evinced by an
application then made to him to allow himself to
run for the Legislature. He consented, though
surprised at the request, and polled a vote considerably in advance of other candidates of the
same party. In New Salem he polled an almost
unanimous vote, men voting for him without regard to party lines. Still, he was defeated. A
brief speech which he made during the canvass
has been preserved, and, as it is characteristic, I
quote it:

"GENTLEMEN AND FELLOW-CITIZENS: I pre-
sume you all know who I am. I am humble
Abraham Lincoln. I have been solicited by

many friends to become a candidate for the Legislature. My politics are short and sweet, like the old woman's dance. I am in favor of a national bank. I am in favor of the internal improvement system and a high protective tariff. These are my sentiments and political principles. If elected, I shall be thankful; if not, it will be all the same."

It will be seen that Mr. Lincoln had cast in his lot with the Whig party—the party of whom Henry Clay was at that time the most distinguished representative, and for whom the young man had a strong admiration.

The great problem of how he was to make his living had not yet been solved by young Lincoln. Dr. Holland is our authority for the statement that he seriously took into consideration the project of learning the blacksmith's trade. An opportunity, however, offered for him to buy out a stock of goods owned by a man of Radford, in connection with a man named Berry. This supplied him employment for a time, but not of a profitable nature, for his partner proved a hindrance rather than a help, and failure ensued. Lincoln was in-volved in debt, and it was six years before he

freed himself from his obligations. About this
time he received his first political appointment—
that of postmaster—from the administration of
General Jackson. It brought in very little rev-
enue, but gave him a privilege which he valued
of reading all the newspapers which came to the
office. The office seemed to have been conducted
in free and easy style. When the young postmaster had occasion to go out he closed the office
and carried off the mail matter in his hat.

When his store was closed permanently, young
Lincoln received an offer from the surveyor of
Sangamon County to undertake all his work in
the immediate neighborhood of New Salem.
Though Lincoln knew nothing of surveying,
either practically or theoretically, he qualified
himself for the work, procured a compass and
chain, and went to work. It is an interesting
proof of the young surveyor's thoroughness that,
in spite of his inadequate preparation, the accuracy of his surveys has never been called in question.

Two years later Lincoln ran again for the Legislature, and this time he succeeded. Among his
colleagues was Major John T. Stuart, a prosper-

ous lawyer of Springfield. He was a previous acquaintance of young Lincoln, and their present companionship strengthened the interest of the older man in his struggling young friend.

"Why don't you study law?" he asked Lincoln.

"Because I am poor; I have no money to buy the necessary books," said Abe.

"Have you ever thought of following the profession?"

"Yes, I have already read law some."

"I believe you would succeed. If books are all you need, I have a large law library and will lend you what you need."

Abe's face lighted up with pleasure.

"You are very kind," he said, "and I will take you at your word. When can I have the books?"

"Whenever you will call for them."

This was not an offer which young Lincoln could afford to slight. At the close of the canvass he walked to Springfield, called at the office of his friend Stuart, and returned to New Salem with a load of books, which he forthwith began to read and study.

"Abe's progress in the law," says Mr. Lamon,

" was as surprising as the intensity of his application to study. He never lost a moment that
might be improved. It is even said that he read
and recited to himself on the road and by the
wayside, as he came down from Springfield with
the books he had borrowed from Stuart. The
first time he went up he had ' mastered ' forty
pages of Blackstone before he got back. It was
not long until, with his restless desire to be doing
something practical, he began to turn his acqui-
sitions to account in forwarding the business of
his neighbors. He wrote deeds, contracts, notes,
and other legal papers, for them, ' using a small
dictionary and an old form-book '; pettifogged
incessantly before the justice of the peace,
and probably assisted that functionary in the
administration of justice as much as he benefited his own clients. This species of country
student practice was entered upon very early,
and kept up until long after he was a distinguished man in the Legislature. But in all this
he was only trying himself; as he was not admitted to the bar until 1837, he did not regard it
as legitimate practice, and never charged a penny
for his services."

Young Lincoln took part in the legislative work of the first session during which he served as a member, but did not push himself forward. He listened and took notes of what was done, and how it was done. He was assigned to an honorable place on the Committee on Public Accounts and Expenditures. It was about this time that he saw for the first time Stephen A. Douglas, with whom he was in after years to be associated in the memorable canvass for the Senatorship. Douglas, who was only about five feet in height, was also slender, and in personal appearance presented a striking contrast to the long-legged young legislator who overtopped him by more than a foot.

"He is the smallest man I ever saw," said Lincoln.

Douglas filled up as he grew older, till he came to deserve the title by which he was so long known, of "The Little Giant." He was not at that time a member of the Legislature, but was a successful candidate for the position of District Attorney for the district in which he lived. Unlike Lincoln, he was not a Western man by birth, having been born and "raised" in Vermont. In fact he had only come West during the previous year; but he was not a man to hide his light under a bushel, and soon worked himself into prominence in his new home. Two years later, in 1838, Douglas, as well as Lincoln, was elected to the Legislature, and they served together. In public life, therefore, Lincoln preceded Douglas by two years, but the latter advanced much more rapidly and became a man of national reputation, while Lincoln was still comparatively obscure.

CHAPTER X.

A CASE IN COURT

WE are told by Mr. Lamon, that Mr. Lincoln got his license as an attorney early in 1837, and commenced practice regularly as a lawyer in the town of Springfield, in March of that year. It is with this place that his name was associated for the remainder of his life. Though it contained at that time less than two thousand inhabitants, it was a town of considerable importance. The list of the local bar contained the names of several men of ability and reputation. Stephen A. Douglas, already referred to, was public prosecutor in 1836. Judge Stephen T Logan was on the bench of the Circuit Court. There was John T. Stuart also, who had recommended young Lincoln to become a lawyer, and was now his partner.

The law office of Stuart and Lincoln was in the second story above the court-room, in Hoffman's Row. It was small and poorly furnished. Lincoln slept in the office, and boarded with Hon. William Butler, who appears to have been a politician and wire-puller.

At last, then, after a youth of penury, a long hand-to-hand struggle with privations in half a dozen different kinds of business, we find our hero embarked in the profession which, for the remainder of his life, he owned as mistress. He is twenty-eight years of age, with some legislative experience, but a mere novice in law. But he was ambitious, and in spite of his scanty equipment as regards book-knowledge, he made up his mind to succeed, and he did succeed.

Though I am thereby anticipating matters, I propose to relate an incident of his law practice which I find quoted in "Raymond's History" of Lincoln's Administrations, from the *Cleveland Leader*. It illustrates not merely Mr. Lincoln's methods and shrewdness as a lawyer, but also his fidelity to friends.

This is the story:

"Some four years since, the eldest son of Mr. Lincoln's old friend, the chief supporter of his widowed mother—the good old man having some time previously passed from earth—was arrested on a charge of murder. A young man had been killed during a riotous *mêlée* in the night time at a camp-meeting, and one of his associates stated that the death-wound was inflicted by young Armstrong. A preliminary examination was gone into, at which the accuser testified so positively, that there seemed no doubt of the guilt of the prisoner, and therefore he was held for trial.

"As is too often the case, the bloody act caused an undue degree of excitement in the public mind. Every improper incident in the life of the prisoner—each act which bore the least semblance of rowdyism—each school-boy quarrel—was suddenly remembered and magnified, until they pictured him as a fiend of the most horrible hue. As these rumors spread abroad they were received as gospel truth, and a feverish desire for vengeance seized upon the infatuated populace, whilst only prison bars prevented a horrible death at the hands of the populace. The events were heralded in the county papers, painted in the highest colors, accompanied by rejoicing over the certainty of punishment being meted out to the guilty party. The prisoner, overwhelmed by the circumstances in which he found himself placed, fell into a melancholy condition bordering on despair, and the widowed mother, looking through her tears, saw no cause for hope from earthly aid.

"At this juncture the widow received a letter from Mr. Lincoln, volunteering his services in an effort to save the youth from the impending stroke. Gladly was his aid accepted, although it seemed impossible for even his sagacity to prevail in such a desperate case ; but the heart of the attorney was in his work, and he set about it with a will which knew no such word as fail. Feeling that the poisoned condition of the public mind was such as to preclude the possibility of impanelling an impartial jury in the court having jurisdiction, he procured a change of venue and a postpone-ment of the trial. He then went studiously to work, unravelling the history of the case, and sat-isfied himself that his client was the victim of malice, and that the statements of the accuser were a tissue of falsehoods.

"When the trial was called on, the prisoner, pale and emaciated, with hopelessness written on every feature, and accompanied by his half-hoping, half-despairing mother—whose only hope was in a mother's belief of her son's innocence, in the justice of the God she worshipped, and in the noble counsel, who, without hope of fee or reward upon earth, had undertaken the cause—took his seat in the prisoners' box, and, with a 'stony firmness,' listened to the reading of the indictment.

" Lincoln sat quietly by, whilst the large body of auditors looked on him as though wondering what he could say in defence of one whose guilt they looked upon as certain. The examination of the witnesses for the State was begun, and a well-arranged mass of evidence, circumstantial and positive, was introduced, which seemed to impale the prisoner beyond the possibility of extrication.

" The counsel for the defense propounded but few questions, and those of a character which excited no uneasiness on the part of the prosecutor —merely, in most cases, requiring the main witnesses to be definite as to time and place. When the evidence of the prosecution was ended, Lincoln introduced a few witnesses, to remove some erroneous impressions in regard to the previous character• of his client, who, though somewhat rowdyish, had never been known to commit a

vicious act; and to show that a greater degree of
ill-feeling existed between the accuser and the accused than between the accused and the deceased.

" The prosecutor felt that the case was a clear
one, and his opening speech was brief and formal.   Lincoln arose, while a deathly silence per-
vaded the vast audience, and, in a clear and moderate tone, began his argument.   Slowly and carefully he reviewed the testimony, pointing out the
hitherto unobserved discrepancies in the statements of the principal witness.   That which had
seemed plain and plausible he made to appear
crooked as a serpent's path.   The witness had
stated that the affair took place at a certain hour
in the evening, and that, by the brightly shining
moon, he saw the prisoner inflict the death-blow
with a slung-shot.   Mr. Lincoln showed that at
the hour referred to, the moon had not yet appeared above the horizon, and, consequently, the
whole tale was a fabrication.

" An almost instantaneous change seemed to
have been wrought in the minds of his auditors,
and the verdict of 'not guilty' was at the end of
every tongue.   But the advocate was not content
with this intellectual achievement.   His whole

being had for months been bound up in this work
of gratitude and mercy, and as the lava of the
overcharged crater bursts from its imprisonment,
so great thoughts and burning words leaped forth
from the soul of the eloquent Lincoln. He drew
a picture of the perjurer so horrid and ghastly,
that the accuser could sit under it no longer, but
reeled and staggered from the court-room, whilst
the audience fancied they could see the brand
upon his brow. Then in words of thrilling pathos,
Lincoln appealed to the jurors as fathers of some
who might become fatherless, and as husbands of
wives who might be widowed, to yield to no previous impressions, no ill-founded prejudice, but to
do his client justice; and as he alluded to the
debt of gratitude which he owed the boy's sire,
tears were seen to fall from many eyes unused to
weeping.

"It was near night when he concluded by saying that if justice were done, as he believed it
would be,—before the sun should set,—it would
shine upon his client a free man.

"The jury retired, and the court adjourned for
the day. Half an hour had not elapsed, when,
as the officers of the court and the volunteer at-

torney sat at the tea-table of their hotel, a messenger announced that the jury had returned to their seats. All repaired immediately to the court-house, and whilst the prisoner was being brought from the jail, the court-room was filled to overflowing with citizens from the town.

"When the prisoner and his mother entered, silence reigned as completely as though the house were empty. The foreman of the jury, in answer to the usual inquiry from the court, delivered the verdict of 'NOT GUILTY!' The widow dropped into the arms of her son, who lifted her up, and told her to look upon him as before, free and innocent. Then with the words, 'Where is Mr. Lincoln?' he rushed across the room, and grasped the hand of his deliverer, whilst his heart was too full for utterance. Lincoln turned his eyes toward the west, where the sun still lingered in view, and then, turning to the youth, said: 'It is not yet sundown, and you are free.' I confess that my cheeks were not wholly unwet by tears, and I turned from the affecting scene. As I cast a glance behind, I saw Abraham Lincoln obeying the Divine injunction by comforting the widowed and fatherless."

When a lawyer can so bravely and affectionately rescue the innocent from the machinations of the wicked, we feel that he is indeed the exponent and representative of a noble profession. It is unfortunate that lawyers so often lend themselves to help iniquity, and oppress the weak. Mr. Lincoln always did his best when he felt that Right and Justice were on his side. When he had any doubts on this point, he lost all his enthusiasm and his courage, and labored mechanically. He believed in justice, and would not willingly act on the wrong side. On one occasion he discovered that he had been deceived by his client, and informed his associate lawyer that he (Lincoln) would not make the plea. His associate, therefore, did so, and to Lincoln's surprise gained a verdict. Convinced, nevertheless, that his client was wrong, he would not accept any part of the handsome fee of nine hundred dollars, which he paid. Only an honest and high-minded lawyer would have acted thus.

CHAPTER XI.

PRACTICING law in those days, and in that region, had some peculiar features. It was the custom for lawyers to "ride the circuit," that is, to accompany the judges from one country-town to another, attending to such business as might offer, in different sections of the State. Railroads had not yet found their way out so far West, and the lawyer was wont to travel on horseback, stopping at cabins on the way to eat and sleep, and, in brief, to "rough it." One brought up like Lincoln was not likely to shrink from any hardships which this might entail. Indeed, it is likely that, upon the whole, he enjoyed it, and that these journeys increased his natural shrewdness and knowledge of human nature, and furnished him with no inconsiderable part of the apposite stories which he was wont to quote in later years.

Here is an incident which will amuse my readers. It is told by Mr. Francis E. Willard: "In one of my temperance pilgrimages through Illinois, I met a gentleman who was the companion in a dreary ride which Lincoln made in a light wagon, going the rounds of a Circuit Court where he had clients to look after. The weather was rainy, the road heavy with mud of the Southern Illinois pottery, never to be imagined as to its blackness and profundity by him who has not seen it, and assuredly needing no description to jostle the memory of one who has. Lincoln enlivened the way with anecdote and recital, for few indeed were the incidents that relieved the tedium of the trip.

"At last, in wallowing through a 'slough' of the most approved Western manufacture, they came upon a poor shark of a hog, who had succumbed to gravitation, and was literally fast in the mud. The lawyers commented on the poor creature's pitiful condition, and drove on. About half a mile was laboriously gone over, when Lincoln suddenly exclaimed: 'I don't know how you feel about it, but I've got to go back and pull that hog out of the slough.'

"His comrade laughed, thinking ؛ merely a joke; but what was his surprise when Lincoln dismounted, left him to his reflections, and, striding slowly back, like a man on stilts, picking his way as his long walking implements permitted, he grappled with the drowning hog, dragged him out of the ditch, left him on its edge to recover his strength, slowly measured off the distance back to his buggy, and the two men drove off as if nothing had happened."

This little incident is given to show that Mr. Lincoln did not confine his benevolence to his own race, but could put himself to inconvenience to relieve the sufferings of an inferior animal. In fact, his heart seemed to be animated by the spirit of kindness, and this is one of the most important respects in which I am glad to hold him out as an example to the young. Emulate that tenderness of heart which led him to sympathize with " the meanest thing that breathes," and, like him, you will win the respect and attachment of the best men and women!

The young lawyer, successful as he was in court, did not make money as fast as some of his professional associates. One reason I have already given—he would not willingly exert his power on the wrong side. Moreover, he was modest, and refrained from exorbitant charges, and he was known at times to remit fees justly due when his client was unfortunate. One day he met a client who had given him a note, nearly due, for professional services.

"Mr. Lincoln," he said, "I have been thinking of that note I owe you. I don't see how I am to meet it. I have been disabled by an explosion, and that has affected my income."

"I heard of your accident," said Lincoln, "and I sympathize with you deeply. As to the note, here it is."

"But I can not meet it at present."

"I don't want you to. Take it, and destroy it. I consider it paid."

No doubt many lawyers would have done the same, but it so happened that Lincoln was at that moment greatly in need of money, and was obliged to defer a journey on that account. It was not out of his abundance, but out of his poverty, that he gave.

As to his professional methods, they were peculiar. He was always generous to an opponent.

Instead of contesting point by point, he often yielded more than was claimed, and excited alarm in the breast of his client. But when this was done, he set to work and stated his own view of the case so urgently that the strength of his opponent's position was undermined, his arguments torn to pieces, and the verdict secured. He was remarkably fair, and stated his case so clearly that no juror of fair intelligence could fail to understand him.

It has already been said that Mr. Lincoln had a partner. It is a proof of his scrupulous honesty that when upon his circuits he tried any cases that were never entered at the office, he carefully set aside a part of the remuneration for the absent partner, who otherwise would never have known of them, and might be supposed hardly entitled to a share of the fees.

For the following anecdote, in further illustration of Mr. Lincoln's conscientiousness in money matters, I am indebted to Mr. Frank B. Carpenter's very interesting little volume, entitled "Six Months at the White House": "About the time Mr. Lincoln came to be known as a successful lawyer, he was waited upon by a lady who held a real-estate claim which she desired to have him prosecute,—putting into his hands, with the necessary papers, a check for two hundred and fifty dollars as a retaining fee. Mr. Lincoln said he would look the case over, and asked her to call again the next day. Upon presenting herself, Mr. Lincoln told her that he had gone through the papers very carefully, and he must tell her frankly that there was not a 'peg' to hang her claim upon, and he could not conscientiously advise her to bring an action. The lady was satisfied, and, thanking him, rose to go. 'Wait,' said Mr. Lincoln, fumbling in his vest pocket; 'here is the check you left with me.' 'But, Mr. Lincoln,' returned the lady, 'I think you have earned *that.*' 'No, no,' he responded, handing it back to her, 'that would not be right. I can't take *pay* for doing my duty.'"

I must find a place here for one of Mr. Lincoln's own stories, relating to a professional adventure, which must have amused him. Mr. Carpenter is my authority here also:

"When I took to the law I was going to court one morning, with some ten or twelve miles of bad road before me, when ———— overtook me in his wagon.

"'Hello, Lincoln!' said he; 'going to the court-house? Come get in, and I will give you a seat.'

"Well, I got in, and ———— went on reading his papers. Presently the wagon struck a stump on one side of the road; then it hopped off to the other. I looked out and saw the driver was jerking from side to side in his seat; so said I, 'Judge, I think your coachman has been taking a drop too much this morning.'

"'Well, I declare, Lincoln,' said he, 'I should not much wonder if you are right, for he has nearly upset me half a dozen times since starting.'

"So, putting his head out of the window, he shouted: 'Why, you infernal scoundrel, you are drunk!'

"Upon which, pulling up his horses, and turning round with great gravity, the coachman said: 'Bedad! but that's the first rightful decision your Honor has given for the last twelve months.'"

Mr. Lincoln's law partnership with Mr. Stuart was of brief duration. It was dissolved in 1840,

and in the same year he formed a new partnership with Judge S. T. Logan, a lawyer of learning and ability.

In 1842 he formed another partnership, of a
still more important character. He married Miss
Mary Todd on the 4th of November of that year.
Miss Todd belonged to a family of social prominence, and it is a matter of interest that, before
marrying Mr. Lincoln, she is said to have had an
opportunity of marrying another person, whose
name was mentioned for the Presidency years before Mr. Lincoln's. I refer to Hon. Stephen A.
Douglas, who is said to have been an unsuccessful
suitor for the hand of Miss Todd.

Six months after marriage, in a private letter
written to an intimate friend, Mr. Lincoln refers
thus to his domestic arrangements: "We are not
keeping house," he writes, "but boarding at the
Globe Tavern, which is very well kept by a widow
lady of the name of Beck. Our rooms are the
same Dr. Wallace occupied there, and boarding
only costs four dollars a week."

Abraham Lincoln had reached the age of thirty-three years before he ventured to marry. Circumstances had until then proved unfavorable, for

his struggle with poverty had been unusually protracted. Now, however, he was settled both mat-
rimonially and professionally, and the most important part of his life, for which he had been so
long preparing, may be said to have fairly begun

CHAPTER XII.

I HAVE already told my readers something of Mr. Lincoln as a lawyer. I may add that he stood high in the estimation of his professional brethren. "For my single self," says one, " I have for a quarter of a century regarded Mr. Lincoln as one of the finest lawyers I ever knew, and of a professional bearing so high-toned and honorable as justly, and without derogating from the claims of others, entitling him to be presented to the profession as a model well worthy of the closest imitation."

Now these are general terms, and do not show us how the young lawyer who had risen step by step from the hardest physical labor to an honorable position at the bar, looked and spoke. Fortunately Judge Drummond, of Chicago, gives us a graphic picture of him,—and I am glad to quote it:

"With a voice by no means pleasant, and, indeed, when excited, in its shrill tones almost disagreeable; without any of the personal graces of the orator; without much in the outward man indicating superiority of intellect; without great quickness of perception—still, his mind was so vigorous, his comprehension so exact and clear, and his judgment so sure, that he easily mastered the intricacies of his profession, and became one of the ablest reasoners and most impressive speakers at our bar. With a probity of character known of all, with an intuitive insight into the human heart, with a clearness of statement which was itself an argument, with uncommon power and felicity of illustration,—often, it is true, of a plain and homely kind—and with that sincerity and earnestness of manner which carried conviction, he was, perhaps, one of the most successful jury lawyers we have ever had in the State. He always tried a case fairly and honestly. He never intentionally misrepresented the evidence of a witness or the argument of an opponent. He met both squarely, and if he could not explain the one or answer the other, substantially admitted it. He never misstated the law according to his own intelligent view of it."

I hope my young readers will not skip this statement, but read it carefully, because it will show them the secret of the young lawyer's success. *He inspired confidence !* He was not constantly trying to gain the advantage by fair means if possible, but at any rate to gain it. He wanted justice to triumph, however it affected his own interests. I wish there were more such lawyers. The law would then lose much of the odium which unprincipled practitioners bring upon it.

Let us look in upon Mr. Lincoln as he sits in his plain office, some morning. He is writing busily, when a timid knock is heard at his door.

"Come in!" he says, his pen still moving rapidly over the paper before him.

The door opens slowly, and an old woman, bending under the burden of seventy-five years, enters, and stands irresolutely at the entrance.

"Mr. Lincoln!" she says in a quivering voice.

As these accents reach him, Mr. Lincoln woke up hastily, and seeing the old lady hastily undoubles himself, and draws forward a chair.

"Sit down, my good lady!" he says. "Do you wish to see me on business?"

"Yes, sir."

"Tell me what I can do for you?" and he fixes his eyes on the frail old woman, showing a respect and consideration for her, poor as she evidently is, which a rich client might not so readily receive.

Encouraged by the kindness of her reception she told her story. She was entitled to a pension, as it appeared, on account of her husband, who had fought in the Revolutionary war. This pension she had secured through the agency of a certain pension agent, but he had charged her the exorbitant sum of two hundred dollars for collecting her claim. This was a heavy tax upon the poor old woman with her limited means, and she was likely to be little better off for her pension if she should be compelled to pay this money.

"Two hundred dollars! That is shameful!" said the sympathetic lawyer. "Who is this agent?"

She told him.

"Do you live in Springfield?"

"No sir."

"Are you in need of money?" he inquired delicately.

"Yes, sir, The agent has kept back what he has collected, and "——

"I see. We will try to bring him to terms."

"Oh, sir if you can help me——" said the old lady, hopefully.

"I will do my best. Here is some money for your immediate wants. Now I will ask you a few questions, and we will see what we can do for you."

Mr. Lincoln immediately commenced suit against the agent to recover a portion of the money which he had withheld. In his address to the jury he did not omit to allude to the patriotism of the dead husband, and the poverty of his widow, and no doubt castigated in fitting terms the unfeeling rapacity of the claim agent. He gained the suit, and compelled the fellow to disgorge one hundred dollars, which he had the pleasure of paying over to his aged client.

Meanwhile he was pleasantly situated. His income would now allow him to live in comfortable style. He established himself in a pleasant two-story house, built after a fashion quite com-

mon in New England, with a room on each side
of the front door, and an extension in the rear.
It was situated at the corner of two streets, and
though neither costly nor sumptuous, might be
considered a palace when contrasted with the
rude cabins in which his earlier years were passed.

Four children were born to him, and their
childish ways were a source of constant enjoy-
ment, when he returned to his home, weary or
perplexed. One of these, Willie, died after his
father became President; the youngest, best
known as Tad, who was the pet of the White
House, is also dead, and only the eldest, Robert
Todd, now Secretary of War, survives. It is
said that he was a most indulgent father, and
governed by Love alone. His own father had
often been stern and rough, but Abraham Lincoln's nature was full of a deep tenderness for
all things weak, small, or in distress, and he could
not find it in his heart to be harsh or stern at
home.

On pleasant summer mornings the young lawyer, with his tall figure, might have been seen
drawing one of his children to and fro along the
sidewalk in a child's wagon. "Without hat or

coat, and wearing a pair of rough shoes, his hands behind him holding to the tongue of the wagon, and his tall form bent forward to accommodate himself to the service, he paced up and down the walk, forgetful of everything around him, and intent only on some subject that absorbed his mind." A young man, who as a boy used to see him thus occupied, admits that he used to wonder "how so rough and plain a man could live in so respectable a house."

I once asked a lady who for a considerable time lived opposite Mr. Lincoln, at Springfield, whether he was really as plain as his pictures all represented him.

" I never saw one of his pictures that did not flatter him," she answered.

" My oldest son was a companion and playfellow of Mr. Lincoln's younger boys," she continued, "and was in and out of his house a dozen times a day. He was a very quiet man. He used to stay at home in the evening, and read or meditate, but Mrs. Lincoln was of a gayer temperament, and cared more for company."

Mr. Lincoln was always a thoughtful man, and though amid social surroundings he could tell a droll story with a humorous twinkle of the eye, his features in repose were grave and even melancholy. As he walked along the street, he often seemed abstracted, and would pass his best friends without recognizing them. Even at the table he was often self-absorbed, and ate his food mechanically, but there was nothing in his silence to dull or make uncomfortable those around him. After a time he would arise from his silence, and make himself companionable as he was always able to do, and lead conversation into some channel in which members of his family could take part.

CHAPTER XIII.

ABRAHAM LINCOLN's professional success di. not fill the measure of his ambition. It certainly was a great step upward from the raw-boned, ragged, barefooted lad to the prosperous lawyer, and our hero, if I may so call him, doubtless felt complacent when he considered the change in his position and surroundings. I may take occasion to say here that Abe—to return to the name which he did not wholly lay aside when he emerged from boyhood and youth—never put on airs because of his elevation, nor looked down upon the humble relatives whom he had left behind. Whenever in his journeyings he found himself near the residence of any of his poorer relations, he took special pains to visit them, and, if possible, to stay with them. Often he pressed upon them money when they appeared to need it—not

8   (113)

with the air of a liberal patron, but with straight-forward friendliness and cordiality. Once when he was urged to remain at the hotel with his professional friends, instead of making a call upon an aged aunt, he said:

"Why, aunt's heart would be broken if I should leave town without calling upon her."

Let me add that this call required something more than ordinary good-natured consideration, for the aunt in question lived several miles away, and her nephew had no horse at his command, but walked all the way. I am very glad to call the attention of all my young friends to this admirable trait in the character of President Lincoln. I wish it were more common. I am sure we all admire the boy or girl who is always thoughtful of the feelings and happiness of older relatives.

But to return from this digression, let me repeat that Mr. Lincoln had other aspirations than to succeed as a lawyer. It has been said that nine out of ten American boys cherish a vague ambition to become President. This is plainly an exaggeration, but it is certain that a large number entertain the hope of some day entering public

life, either as legislator or Congressman, or at any
rate as a salaried officer. That is one reason why
there is such a horde of office-seekers swarming
to our National or State capitals, ambitious to
earn a living at the expense of the Government.
Some throw up good mercantile positions and
spend months in the attempt to secure a position
as department clerk, foreign consul, or poorly-
paid postmaster.

Abraham Lincoln's ambition was of a more
elevated character. He had a pardonable ambition to take part in the government of his country, not for the sake of the position so much, as
because he felt within himself the capacity to
shape legislation to worthy ends. He was not
alone in this idea. His fellow-citizens had gauged
him and felt that he was fit to represent them. I
have already spoken of his service in the State
Legislature; but he was only preparing himself
there for a wider arena. In 1846 he received the
nomination for Congress from the Sangamon district. Now it was not the fashion in those days
for a candidate to remain quietly at home pursu-
ing his business as usual while waiting for the
popular verdict. It is perhaps the more dignified

course to pursue, but it would not have elected Mr. Lincoln. He understood at once that he would have to "stump" the district. I need hardly explain to my young readers what this means. He must visit the principal towns and villages, and address public meetings of the people on political subjects of present interest, explaining clearly how he stood, and how he proposed to vote if elected.

For this service Lincoln was very well fitted. He had a vigorous Saxon style, and he knew how to make things clear even to the humblest intellect. Then, again, he possessed a fund of homely, but pertinent stories, which often produced more effect than a protracted argument. However, he was not limited to such means of influencing his audiences. He had a logical mind and a happy faculty of stating things clearly and precisely, so as to convince the reason as well as to persuade the judgment.

There was no lack of topics on which to speak. The country was in an excited state. Texas had been admitted to the Union, war with Mexico had succeeded, and opinions were divided as to the wisdom of entering upon it. The Whig party, of which Mr. Lincoln was a member, considered it unnecessary and unjustifiable. So also did the Anti-Slavery party, then coming into existence. Many of my young readers have doubtless read the "Biglow Papers," by our eminent poet and diplomatist, James Russell Lowell, and have enjoyed the quaint and pungent sarcasm with which he assails those who were instrumental in bringing on this ill-advised war. I speak of it as ill-advised, for, though some of the results, notably the acquisition of California, have proved beneficial, the object for which the war was commenced and waged was far from commendable. The tariff also had been recently repealed, and the result was a disturbance of the business interests of the country. Clearly, Congress and the country had plenty to talk about and plenty to legislate about.

Mr. Lincoln's speeches in this "stumping' tour have not been preserved, but we have every reason to believe that he did himself credit, and maintained the reputation he had already acquired as a strong and forcible speaker. The best evidence we can adduce is his triumphant election by much more than the usual party vote

Even Mr. Clay, with all his popularity as a Presidential candidate in 1844, received a majority less by about six hundred than were given to Abraham Lincoln in his contest for a seat in Congress.

So we chronicle one more step in the upward progress of the young rail-splitter. On the 6th of December, 1847, he took his seat in the Thirtieth Congress, as a Representative from his adopted State of Illinois. At the same time his future rival, Stephen A. Douglas, took his seat in the United States Senate, representing the same State. Lincoln was the tallest man among the nearly three hundred who sat in the House. Douglas was the shortest man in the Senate. Both were to achieve high distinction, and to fill a remarkable place in the history of their country. To Lincoln distinction came with slower steps, but he was destined to mount higher and achieve a more enduring fame. Of the two, Douglas was more of a politician, and he was more ready to sacrifice principle in the interest of personal ambition. Years later they were to stump the State as competitors for Senatorial honors in a memorable canvass, and still later to be rival candidates for the Presidency. In the first, Douglas secured the election; in the second, Lincoln. It is to the credit of Douglas that when the last contest was decided, and his competitor, who had secured the prize for which he had labored earnestly for years, was about to take his seat, at a time when the first faint rumblings of the Civil War were being heard, and well-grounded fears were entertained for the safety of the President-elect, he laid aside all the bitterness of personal feelings and disappointed ambition, and rode with his old rival to the capital on Inauguration Day, content to share any personal risk in which he might be placed.

The closing period of the life of Douglas does him great credit. It shows him in the character of patriot, rather than as politician. In former years he had been willing to make concessions to the slave power, in order to further his own chances of the Presidential succession. Now, when civil war was imminent and the integrity of the Government was menaced, he forgot the politician and stood side by side with Lincoln for the preservation of the Government which he had so long served. It was a source of sincere regret to Abraham Lincoln that Douglas should have

been removed by death so early in the Civil War.
It removed from him a staunch friend and supporter, whose influence was all the greater because he was perhaps the most prominent member of the opposition.

I have a personal remembrance of Mr. Douglas, to whom i was introduced on the occasion of
a visit to Massachusetts. Short as he was, he had
a dignified and impressive presence, and his mas-
sive figure well entitled him to the name by which
he was so commonly known, "The Little Giant."
He was not destined to achieve the object of his
ambition, but he will long be remembered as an
influential actor in our political history.

CHAPTER XIV.

THE backwoods-boy is now in Congress. He is one of the law-makers of the nation, and is an equal associate of eminent statesmen gathered from all parts of the country.

Let us look about us as we enter the old Hall of Representatives, and see into what company the backwoods-boy has come.

In the Speaker's chair sits a dignified-looking man, an accomplished parliamentarian, whom friends and opponents alike concede to be amply competent to discharge the duties of his high place—this is Robert C. Winthrop, of Massachusetts, living still in a dignified and honored old age. Among the notable members of this Congress were John Quincy Adams, who had already been President, but who was willing notwithstanding to serve his country in an humble place; George Ashmun, also representing Massachusetts; Jacob Collamer; Alexander H. Stephens, afterward Vice-President of the Southern Confederacy; Robert Toombs; Andrew Johnson, afterward associated with Mr. Lincoln as Vice-President, and upon whose shoulders fell the mantle of his lamented chief; Marsh, Truman Smith, Wilmot, Rhett, Giddings, and others, whose names were already conspicuous. This will give some idea of the personnel of the House; while in the Senate chamber, at the other end of the Capitol, Webster, Calhoun, Dix, Dickinson, Hale, Crittenden, and Corwin lent weight and dignity to that co-ordinate legislative branch of the Government.

Such were the men with whom the young Western member was to share the labors of legislation. Time has given to some of them a fame which they did not then possess. Their successors of our day may, after the lapse of a generation, bear names as weighty; but I am afraid we shall look in vain for successors of Webster, Calhoun, John Quincy Adams, A. H. Stephens, and Crittenden.

The question will occur to my young readers, What part did Abraham Lincoln take in the national councils? Was he a cipher, an obscure member, simply filling his seat and drawing his pay, or did he take an active part in the business of the session? I will say in answer, that he was by no means a cipher. Though he did not aspire to be a leader—for in a new member that would have been in bad taste—he was always ready to take part when he felt called upon to do so, and his vote and words were such as he would not in after years have felt it necessary to recall or apologize for.

It is interesting to know that he arrayed himself with Mr. Giddings in favor of abolishing slavery in the District of Columbia. Mr. Giddings little suspected that the plain member from Illinois, whose co-operation he had secured, was to be the instrument under Providence of abolishing slavery, not only in the District of Columbia, but throughout the land.

But slavery was not at that time the leading political question of the day. Parties were divided upon the subject of the Mexican war. While opposed to the war, Mr. Lincoln was in favor of voting for the necessary supplies and appropriations, and he took care, in an elaborate speech, to explain his position. He felt that it was his duty as a citizen and a patriot to see that the army which had been sent to Mexico should be properly sustained; but he did not for a moment concede that the war was just or necessary. As President Polk saw fit to construe such a vote as a formal approval of his action and of the war, Mr. Lincoln made an elaborate speech in arraignment of his interpretation. As this was Mr. Lincoln's first speech in Congress, I shall make considerable quotations from it, partly to show where he stood on this important question, and partly to prove to my readers that he was no novice, but well qualified for the high position to which he had been elected by the suffrages of his fellow-citizens. I am quite aware that many of my young readers will skip this portion as uninteresting; but I hope that if in after years they are led to read this biography once more, they will count it worth while to read it.

After reviewing and controverting the reasons assigned by the President for the statement that Mexico had invaded our soil, and that therefore 'by the act of the Republic of Mexico a state of war exists between that Government and the United States," Mr. Lincoln proceeds:

"I am now through the whole of the President's evidence; and it is a singuar fact, that if any one should declare the President sent the army into the midst of a settlement of Mexican people who had never submitted, by consent or by force, to the authority of Texas or of the United States, and that *there* and *thereby* the first blood of the war was shed, there is not one word in all the President has said which would either admit or deny the declaration. In this strange omission chiefly consists the deception of the President's evidence—an omission which it does seen to me could scarcely have occurred but by design. My way of living leads me to be about the courts of justice; and there I have sometimes seen a good lawyer struggling for his client's neck, in a desperate case, employing every artifice to work round, befog, and cover up with many words some position pressed upon him by the prosecution, which he *dared* not admit and yet *could* not deny. Party bias may help to make it appear so; but, with all the allowance I can make for such bias, it still does appear to me that just such, and from such necessity, are the President's struggles in this case.

"Some time after my colleague (Mr. Richard
son) introduced the resolutions I have mentioned,
I introduced a preamble, resolution, and interrogatories, intended to draw the President out, if
possible, on this hitherto untrodden ground.   To
show their relevancy, I propose to state my understanding of the true rule for ascertaining the
boundary between Texas and Mexico.   It is that
wherever Texas was *exercising* jurisdiction was
hers; and wherever Mexico was exercising jurisdiction was hers; and that whatever separated
the actual exercise of jurisdiction of the one
from that of the other, was the true boundary
between them.   If, as is probably true, Texas
was exercising jurisdiction along the western
bank of the Nueces, and Mexico was exercising
it along the eastern bank of the Rio Grande;
then neither river was the boundary, but the
uninhabited country between the two was.   The
extent of our territory in that region depended
not on any treaty-fixed boundary (for no treaty
had attempted it), but on revolution.   Any people
anywhere, being inclined and having the power,
have the *right* to rise up and shake off the existing Government, and form a new one that suits

them better. This is a most valuable, a most sacred right—a right which, we hope and believe, is to liberate the world. Nor is this right confined to cases in which the whole people of an existing Government may choose to exercise it. Any portion of such people that *can* may revolutionize and make their own of so much of the territory as they inhabit. More than this, a majority of any portion of such people may revolutionize, putting down a minority, intermingled, or near about them, who may oppose their movements. Such minority was precisely the case of the Tories of our own Revolution. It is a quality of revolutions not to go by old lines or old laws, but to break up both and make new ones. As to the country now in question, we bought it of France in 1803 and sold it to Spain in 1819, according to the President's statement. After this, all Mexico, including Texas, revolutionized against Spain ; and still later, Texas revolutionized against Mexico. In my view, just so far as she carried her revolution by obtaining the *actual*, willing or unwilling, submission of the people, *so far* the country was hers and no further.

"Now, sir, for the purpose of obtaining the

very best evidence as to whether Texas had actu-
ally carried her revolution to the place where the
hostilities of the present war commenced, let the
President answer the interrogatories I proposed,
as before mentioned, or some other similar ones.
Let him answer fully, fairly, and candidly; let
him answer with *facts*, and not with arguments.
Let him remember he sits where Washington sat;
and, so remembering, let him answer as Wash
ington would answer. As a nation *should* not,
and the Almighty *will* not be evaded, so let him
attempt no evasion, no equivocation; and if, so
answering, he can show that the soil was ours
where the first blood of the war was shed—that
it was not within an inhabited country, or, if
within such, that the inhabitants had submitted
themselves to the civil authority of Texas or of
the United States, and that the same is true of the
site of Fort Brown—then I am with him for his
justification. In that case, I shall be most happy
to reverse the vote I gave the other day. I have
a selfish notion for desiring that the President·
may do this; I expect to give some votes in connection with the war, which, without his so doing, will be of doubtful propriety, in my own

judgment, but which will be free from the doubt, if he does so.

"But if he *can not* or *will not* do this—if on any pretense, or no pretense, he shall refuse or omit it—then I shall be fully convinced of what I more than suspect already, that he is deeply conscious of being in the wrong; that he feels the blood of this war, like the blood of Abel, is crying to heaven against him; that he ordered General Taylor into the midst of a peaceful Mexican settlement, purposely to bring on war; that originally having some strong motive — what I will not stop now to give my opinion concerning—to involve the two countries in a war, and trusting to escape scrutiny by fixing the public gaze upon the exceeding brightness of military glory — that attractive rainbow that rises in showers of blood—that serpent's eye that charms to destroy—he plunged into it, and has swept *on* and *on*, till, disappointed in his calculation of the ease with which Mexico might be subdued, he now finds himself he knows not where. How like the half-insane mumbling of a fever dream is the whole war part of the last message! At one time telling us that Mexico has nothing whatever that we can get but territory; at another showing us how we can support the war by levy-ing contributions on Mexico; at one time urging the national honor, the security of the future, the prevention of foreign interference, and even the good of Mexico herself, as among the objects of the war; at another, telling us that 'to reject in-demnity by refusing to accept a cession of terri-tory would be to abandon all our just demands, and to wage the war, bearing all its expenses, *without a purpose or definite object.*'

"So then, the national honor, security of the future, and everything but territorial indemnity, may be considered *no purposes* and *indefinite* ob-jects of the war! But having it now settled that territorial indemnity is the only object, we are urged to seize, by legislation here, all that he was content to take a few months ago, and the whole province of Lower California to boot, and to still carry on the war—to take *all* we are fighting for, and *still* fight on. Again the President is resolv-ed, under all circumstances, to have full territo-rial indemnity for the expenses of the war; but he forgets to tell us how we are to get the *excess* after those expenses shall have surpassed the value of the *whole* of the Mexican territory. So, again, he insists that the separate national existence of Mexico shall be maintained ; but he does not tel. us *how* this can be done after we shall have taken *all* her territory. Lest the questions I here suggest be considered speculative merely, let me be indulged a moment in trying to show they are not.

"The war has gone on some twenty months, for the expenses of which, together with an inconsiderable old score, the President now claims about one-half of the Mexican territory, and that by far the better half, so far as concerns our ability to make anything out of it. It is comparatively uninhabited, so that we could establish land offices in it, and raise money in that way. But the other half is already inhabited, as I understand it, tolerably densely for the nature of the country ; and all its lands, or all that are valuable, already appropriated as private property. How, then, are we to make anything out of these lands with this incumbrance on them, or how remove the incumbrance? I suppose no one will say we should kill the people, or drive them out, or make slaves of them, or even confiscate their property ? How, then, can we make much out of this part of the territory ? If the prosecution of the war has, in expenses, already equalled the *better* half of the country, how long its future prosecution will be in equalling the less valuable half is not a *speculative* but a *practical* question, pressing closely upon us, and yet it is a question which the President seems never to have thought of.

"As to the mode of terminating the war and securing peace, the President is equally wandering and indefinite. First, it is to be done by a more vigorous prosecution of the war in the vital parts of the enemy's country; and, after apparently talking himself tired on this point, the President drops down into a half-despairing tone, and tells us ' that, with a people distracted and divided by contending factions, and a government subject to constant changes, by successive revolutions, *the continued success of our arms may fail to obtain a satisfactory peace.*' Then he suggests the propriety of wheedling the Mexican people to desert the counsels of their own leaders, and, trusting in our protection, to set up a government from which we can obtain a satisfactory peace, telling us that '*this may become the only mode of obtaining such a peace.*' But soon he falls into doubt of this too, and then drops back on to the already abandoned ground of 'more vigorous prosecution.' All this shows that the President is in no wise satisfied with his own positions. First, he takes up one, and, in attempting to argue us into it, he argues himself *out* of it; then seizes another, and goes through the same process; and then, confused at being able to think of nothing new, he snatches up the old one again, which he has some time before cast off. His mind, tasked beyond its power, is running hither and thither, like some tortured creature on a burning surface, finding no position on which it can settle down and be at ease.

" Again, it a singular omission in the message, that it nowhere intimates *when* the President expects the war to terminate. At its beginning, General Scott was, by this same President, driven into disfavor, if not disgrace, for intimating that peace could not be conquered in less than three or four months. But now, at the end of about twenty months, during which time our arms have given us the most splendid successes—every de-

partment and every part, land and water, officers
and privateers, regulars and volunteers, doing all
that men could do, and hundreds of things which
it had ever before been thought that men could
not do; after all this, this same President gives
us a long message without showing us that, *as to
the end*, he has himself even an imaginary con-
ception. As I have before said, he knows not
where he is. He is a bewildered, confounded,
and miserably perplexed man. God grant he may
be able to show that there is not something about
his conscience more painful than all his mental
perplexity?"

It will be seen that, new as he is to the halls of
Congress, Mr. Lincoln speaks with the freedom,
and in the assured tone, of a veteran member. I
have nothing to say as to the sentiments contained
in these extracts. I wished my readers to see
what sort of a speech the Illinois Congressman,
trained in the backwoods, and almost absolutely
without educational advantages, was able to make.
It will be conceded that the result, all things considered, is remarkable. When, twelve years later,
he was nominated for the post of Chief Magistrate, it was a fashion among many, in both po-

litical parties, to speak of him as an obscure member of Congress, who had never attracted any attention during his service in the House. This was not correct. He took a prominent part in legislation of all kinds. and made himself acquainted with whatever subjects came up for consideration.

It has often been said that fact is stranger than fiction, and I am tempted to remark that the new Congressman who so boldly criticised President Polk for his management of the war, was far from dreaming that he himself would be subject to similar attacks when, as President, the management of a far more important war devolved upon him.

CHAPTER XV.

WHEN Mr. Lincoln's first Congressional term expired, he declined to be a candidate for re-election. He was a delegate to the convention that nominated General Taylor for the Presidency, and did what he could to bring about his election. He would have preferred Henry Clay, who was unquestionably far more fit for the position of Chief Magistrate, being an experienced statesman, while Taylor was only a rough soldier; but availability then, as now, controlled the choice of conventions, and Clay was laid aside, failing, like Webster, to reach the Presidency.

My young readers are aware that President Taylor died about a year after his inauguration, and was succeeded by Millard Fillmore, the Vice-President. Mr. Fillmore offered Lincoln the position of Governor of Oregon, then a Territory.

The offer was considered, and might have been accepted but for the opposition of Mrs. Lincoln, who naturally objected to going so far from home and friends. So, for the time, Mr. Lincoln retired from politics, though he by no means ceased to feel an interest in the state of the country. He, like other sagacious statesmen, saw that slavery was to be the rock in the way of national harmony, and we are told by Mr. Lamon, that when coming home to Springfield from the Fremont Court in company with Mr. Stuart, he said : "The time will come when we must all be Democrats or Abolitionists. When that time comes my mind is made up. The slavery question can't be compromised." .

About this time his father, who had lived to see the first political success of his son, was drawing near the end of his life. His latter years had been made comfortable by the pecuniary help freely tendered by his son, who gave, but not out of his abundance. Anxious that his father should have every comfort which his case required, he wrote the following letter, which I quote, because it illustrates not only his solicitude for his family, but also exhibits his faith in his Maker:

"SPRINGFIELD, *January* 12, 1851.

"DEAR BROTHER—On the day before yesterday I received a letter from Harriet, written at Green-up. She says she has just returned from your house, and that father is very low, and will hard-ly recover. She also says that you have written me two letters, and, although I have not answered them, it is not because I have forgotten them, or not been interested about them, but because it ap-peared to me I could write nothing which could do any good. You already know that I desire that neither father nor mother shall be in want of any comfort, either in health or sickness, while they live ; and I feel sure you have not failed to use my name, if necessary, to procure a doctor or anything else for father in his present sickness. My business is such that I could hardly leave home now, if it were not, as it is, that my own wife is sick-a-bed.

"I sincerely hope father may yet recover his health ; but, at all events, tell him to remember to call upon and confide in our great and good and merciful Maker, who will not turn away from him in any extremity. He notes the fall of a sparrow, and numbers the hairs of our heads ; and

He will not forget the dying man who puts his trust in him. Say to him that, if we could meet now, it is doubtful whether it would not be more painful than pleasant, but that, if it be his lot to go now, he will soon have a joyous meeting with loved ones gone before, and where the rest of us, through the help of God, hope ere long to join him.

"Write me again when you receive this.

"Affectionately,

"A. LINCOLN."

The money expended for his father and mother we may be sure that Mr. Lincoln gave cheerfully, and I should have a very poor opinion of him if it were otherwise; but he was also called upon to assist another member of the family who was far less deserving. His step-brother, John Johnston, was a rolling-stone, idle, shiftless, and always hard up. I am going to quote here the greater part of a letter written to this step-brother, because it contains some very practical advice, which most of my young readers will not need, but it may fall under the eye of some one who will be benefited by it. It appears that John had made

application for a loan of eighty dollars. Mr,
Lincoln writes :

" Your request for eighty dollars I do not think ít
best to comply with now. At the various times when
I have helped you a little, you have said to me, ' We
can get along very well now '; but in a very short
time I find you in the same difficulty again. Now
this can only happen by some defect in your conduct; what that defect is, I think I know. You
are not *lazy*, and still you are an *idler*.   I doubt
whether, since I saw you, you have done a good
whole day's work in any one day. You do not
very much dislike to work, and still you do not
work much, merely because it does not seem to
you that you could get much for it.   This habit
of uselessly wasting time is the whole difficulty;
and it is vastly important to you, and still more
so to your children, that you should break the
habit.   It is more important to them because
they have longer to live, and can keep out of an
idle habit before they are in it easier than they
can get out after they are in.

" You are now in need of some money; and
what I propose is, that you should go to work
• tooth and nail for somebody who will give you

money for it. Let father and your boys take
charge of things at home, prepare for a crop, and
make the crop, and you go to work for the best
money, wages, or in discharge of any debt you
owe, that you can get; and, to secure you a fair
reward for your labor, I now promise you that,
for every dollar you will, between this and the
first of next May, get for your own labor, either
in money or your own indebtedness, I will then
give you one other dollar. By this, if you hire yourself at ten dollars a month, from me you will get
ten more, making twenty dollars a month for your
work. In this I do not mean you shall go off to
St. Louis, or the lead mines, or the gold mines in
California; but I mean for you to go at it for the
best wages you can get close to home, in Coles
County. Now, if you will do this, you will be
soon out of debt, and, what is better, you will
have a habit that will keep you from getting into
debt again. But, if I should now clear you out
of debt, next year you would be just as deep in
as ever. You say you would almost give your
place in heaven for seventy or eighty dollars.
Then you value your place in heaven very cheap;
for I am sure you can, with the offer I make, get

the seventy or eighty dollars for four or five
months' work. You say, if I will furnish you
the money, you will deed me the land, and, if
you don't pay me the money back, you will deliver possession. Nonsense! If you can't now
live with the land, how will you then live without it? You have always been kind to me, and
I do not mean to be unkind to you. On the contrary, if you will but follow my advice, you will
find it worth more than eighty times eighty dollars to you."

This was certainly excellent advice, and the
offer was a kind and generous one. But it does
not seem to have convinced the one who received
it, for we find him nursing plans of emigration.
Shiftless people are very apt to think they can
earn a living away from home better than at
home. But the trouble is in themselves, not in
their surroundings. Abraham Lincoln finds it
necessary, under date of November 4, 1851, to
combat this fancy of his step-brother. I shall
not apologize for copying a second letter, and I
hope all my young readers will carefully read and
consider it.

" When I came into Charleston day before yes-

terday, I learned that you are anxious to sell the
land where you live, and move to Missouri. I
have been thinking of this ever since, and can
not but think such a notion is utterly foolish.
What can you do in Missouri better than here?
Is the land any richer? Can you there, any
more than here, raise corn and wheat and oats
without work? Will anybody there, any more
than here, do your work for you? If you intend
to go to work, there is no better place than right
where you are; if you do not intend to go to
work you can not get along anywhere.

"Squirming and crawling about from place to
place can do no good. You have raised no crop
this year; and what you really want is to sell the
land, get the money, and spend it. Part with the
land you have, and my life upon it, you will never
after own a spot big enough to bury you in.
Half you will get for the land you will spend in
moving to Missouri, and the other half you will
eat and drink and wear out, and no foot of land
will be bought. Now, I feel it is my duty to
have no hand in such a piece of foolery. I feel
that it is so even on your own account, and particularly on mother's account. The eastern forty

acres I intend to keep for mother while she lives; if you *will not cultivate it*, it will rent for enough to support her; at least it will rent for something. Her dower in the other two forties she can let you have, and no thanks to me. Now, do not misunderstand this letter; I do not write it in any unkindness—I write it, in order, if possible, to get you to *face* the truth, which truth is, you are destitute because you have idled away all your time. Your thousand pretences for not getting along better are all nonsense : they deceive nobody but yourself. *Go to work* is the only cure in your case."

Nothing can be plainer, or more in accordance with common sense than this advice. Though it was written for the benefit of one person only, I feel that I am doing my young, and possibly some older, readers a service in transferring it to my pages, and commending them to heed it. In my own experience, which is by no means exceptional, I have known many who have been willing to move anywhere, and make any change, for the chance of earning a living more easily. About thirty years ago, a great wave of emigration flowed toward the far Pacific, and men of all callings and professions, including not a few college graduates, put on the miner's humble garb and delved for gold among the mountains and by the river-courses of California. Some came back rich, but in many cases had they been willing to work as hard and live as frugally at the East, they would have fared as well. In this case, perhaps, it was as well to remove where the incentives to work overcame their natural indolence, and awakened their ambition.

In this country, fortunately, there are few places where an industrious man can not get a living, if he is willing to accept such work as falls in his way. This willingness often turns the scale, and converts threatening ruin into prosperity and success. Some years since, I made one of the passengers in a small steamer on Puget Sound. My attention was drawn to a young man, apparently about twenty, who was accompanied by his wife and two young children. They were emigrating from Indiana, I believe. He was evidently an industrious man, and his brown face and hands spoke of labor in the field, and under the summer sun. I entered into conversation, and my new acquaintance told me with perfect cheerfulness that when he arrived at Seattle, he would have just ten dollars left, to keep himself and family till he could secure work.

" How should I feel," I could not help asking myself, " if I were placed in similar circumstances, though I had myself only to provide for ? "

Yet the young man appeared quite undisturbed. He had faith in himself, and in Providence, and borrowed no trouble. I have no doubt he found something to do before his money gave out. He was not one of that shiftless and restless class to whom it is very clear Mr. Lincoln's step-brother belonged. Such men thrive in a new country, and make a living anywhere.

CHAPTER XVI.

MR. LINCOLN had served a term in the House
of Representatives with credit to himself' and
profit to the country. He was regarded as a rising man, and every year made him more prominent. It is not strange that his ambition should
have coveted a seat in the Senate. In 1855 he
was a candidate before the Legislature to succeed
General Shields, but, failing to get the required
number of votes, he counselled his friends to vote
for Judge Trumbull, who was elected. It was a
personal disappointment, for he wished to be
Senator, but in the end it proved to his advantage. A seat in the Senate would have stood in
the way of his later triumph, and some one else
in all probability would have been nominated and
elected President of the United States in 1860.

I have already spoken of Mr. Lincoln's opposition to slavery. He was not an extreme man, and he was never classed with the Abolitionists —that intrepid band who worked early and late, and for years almost without hope, against the colossal system of wrong whose life seemed so entwined with the life of the republic that it looked as if both must fall together. Abraham Lincoln moved slowly. He was not an impulsive man, but took time to form a determination. Even in the war there were many who blamed him for what appeared to be his slowness, but after a while they were led to see that if slow he was sure, and struck only when the time had come.

The ten years before the war were years of political commotion. The "irrepressible conflict" between slavery and the spirit of freedom had commenced, and Abraham Lincoln arrayed himself among the champions of freedom. There was a desperate struggle to introduce slavery into the Territories, so that in course of time more slave States might be added to the Union, and thus the slave system might be strengthened and continue to retain the political ascendency it had possessed for years. The rapid growth of the free Northwest alarmed ˙e slave power, and a counterpoise was required. Northern statesmen who cherished an ambition to be President had notice served upon them that they must help the slave power or forfeit its support. Among those who weakly yielded to this arrogant demand was Stephen A. Douglas. He favored the principle of "squatter sovereignty," permitting the inhabitants of any Territory to establish slavery within its limits if so disposed. In the year 1854, Mr. Lincoln, in a public debate with Mr. Douglas held at Springfield at the State fair, used this significant language :

"My distinguished friend says it is an insult to the emigrants to Kansas and Nebraska to suppose they are not able to govern themselves. We must not slur over an argument of this kind because it tickles the ear. It must be met and answered. I admit that the emigrant to Kansas and Nebraska is able to govern *himself*, but," the speaker rising to his full height, "*I deny his right to govern any other person* WITHOUT THAT PERSON'S CONSENT."

This was but a preliminary skirmish. Four years later came the memorable series of debates between Lincoln and Douglas, each being the nominee of his party for the United States Senate. The platform on which Lincoln stood contained two significant planks, and these furnished the key-note for the speeches called forth by the campaign. I quote them both, and I hope that my young friends will not skip them.

" 3. The present administration has proved recreant to the trusts committed to its hands, and by its extraordinary, corrupt, unjust, and undignified exertions, to give effect to the original intention and purpose of the Kansas-Nebraska bill, by forcing upon the people of Kansas against their will, and in defiance of their known and earnestly-expressed wishes, a constitution recognizing slavery as one of their domestic institutions, it has forfeited all claim to the support of the friends of free men, free labor, and free rights."

" 5. While we deprecate all interference on the part of political organizations with the action of the Judiciary, if such action is limited to its appropriate sphere, yet we can not refrain from expressing our condemnation of the principles and tendencies of the extra judicial opinions of a majority of the Judges of the Supreme Court of the

United States in the matter of Dred Scott, wherein the political heresy is put forth that the Federal Constitution extends slavery into all the Territories of the republic, and so maintains it that neither Congress nor people, through their territorial legislature, can by law abolish it. We hold that Congress possesses sovereign power over the Territories while they remain in a territorial condition, and that it is the duty of the General Government to protect the Territories from the curse of slavery, and to preserve the public domain for the occupation of free men and free labor. And we declare that no power on earth can carry and maintain slavery in the States against the will of the people and the provisions of their constitutions and laws; and we fully endorse the recent decision of the Supreme Court of our own State which declares 'that property in persons is repugnant to the Constitution and laws of Illinois, and that all persons within its jurisdiction are supposed to be free; and that slavery, where it exists, is a municipal regulation without any extra territorial operation.' "

With the other points of difference we are not concerned. Whether slavery should or should not be allowed to extend its blight over the virgin soil of the new Territories, and thus make its final extinction well-nigh impossible: that was the all-important issue, and not Illinois alone, but the country at large, was profoundly interested in the arguments of the two contestants.

Which was likely to win?

It might have been supposed at the outset that Lincoln would find himself overmatched. He was hardly known outside his own State, though he had served two years in Congress. Douglas was a statesman of national reputation. For fifteen years he had been in the thick of the conflict. He was a recognized leader of his party, and already he was looked upon as a probable President at no distant period. In scholastic training he was far ahead of Mr. Lincoln. He was a forcible speaker, an adroit and experienced politician, and his recognized position lent a certain weight to his words which his opponent could not claim.

But, admitting all this, Mr. Douglas found himself confronted by no inferior antagonist. Abraham Lincoln had a strong logical mind, quick to detect sophistry and bold to expose it. He had a fine command of language, a clear and pleasant voice, and a power of sarcasm which he used with powerful execution at times. This is the way in which an intelligent correspondent speaks of his speech at Galesburg:

"For about forty minutes he spoke with a power which we have seldom heard equalled. There was a grandeur in his thoughts, a comprehensiveness in his arguments, and a binding force in his conclusions, which were perfectly irresistible. The vast throng was silent as death, every eye was fixed upon the speaker, and all gave him serious attention. He was the tall man eloquent; his countenance glowed with animation, and his eye glistened with an intelligence that made it lustrous. He was no longer awkward and ungainly; but graceful, bold, and commanding.

"Mr. Douglas had been quietly smoking up to this time, but here he forgot his cigar and listened with anxious attention. When he rose to reply he appeared excited, disturbed, and his second effort seemed to us vastly inferior to his first. Mr. Lincoln had given him a great task, and Mr. Douglas had not time to answer him, even if he had the ability."

Yet there were many points of resemblance be-

tween the two contestants. Both had been cradled in poverty, and had fought their way upward from obscurity to distinction. Douglas had
climbed the higher, but the topmost round of the
ladder on which he had for some time fixed longing eyes, he was destined never to mount. He
had sacrificed much to reach the crowning distinction, but it was not for him. His awkward, un-
graceful opponent, obscure in comparison with
him, was destined to stride past him and sit in the
coveted seat of power. But the smaller prize—
the Senatorship—was won by Douglas, though
Lincoln carried the popular vote.

CHAPTER XVII.

If I were writing a complete and exhaustive biography of Mr. Lincoln, I should be tempted to quote freely from the speeches made by both contestants in the memorable campaign which made Douglas a Senator, and his opponent the next President of the United States. But neither my space, nor the scope of my book, allows this. I will, however, quote, as likely to be of general interest, the personal description of Lincoln given by his distinguished rival:

"In the remarks I have made on this platform," said Judge Douglas, "and the position of Mr. Lincoln upon it, I mean nothing personally disrespectful or unkind to that gentleman. I have known him for nearly twenty-five years. There were many points of sympathy between us when we first got acquainted. We were both comparatively boys, and both struggling with poverty in a strange land. I was a school-teacher in the town of Winchester, and he a flourishing grocery-keeper in the town of Salem. He was more successful in his occupation than I was in mine, and hence more fortunate in this world's goods. Lincoln is one of those peculiar men who perform with admirable skill everything which they undertake. I made as good a school-teacher as I could, and when a cabinet-maker I made a good bedstead and tables, although my old boss said I succeeded better with bureaus and secretaries than with anything else; but I believe that Lincoln was always more successful in business than I, for his business enabled him to get into the Legislature. I met him there, however, and had a sympathy with him, because of the up-hill struggle we both had in life.

"He was then just as good at telling an anecdote as now. He could beat any of the boys in wrestling, or running a foot-race, in pitching quoits, or tossing a copper; could ruin more liquor than all the l oys of the town together, and the dignity and impartiality with which he presided at a horse-race or a fist-fight, excited the admiration and won the praise of everybody that was present and participated. I sympathized with him because he was struggling with difficulties and so was I. Mr. Lincoln served with me in the Legislature in 1836, when we both retired, and he subsided, or became submerged, and he was lost sight of as a public man for some years. In 1846, when Wilmot introduced the celebrated proviso, and the Abolition tornado swept over the country, Lincoln again turned up as a Member of Congress from the Sangamon district. I was then in the Senate of the United States, and was glad to welcome my old friend and companion. While in Congress, he distinguished himself by his opposition to the Mexican war, taking the side of our common enemy against his own country; and when he returned home he found that the indignation of the people followed him everywhere, and he was again submerged, or obliged to retire into private life, forgotten by his former friends."

This sketch of Mr. Lincoln, though apparently friendly, was artfully calculated to stir up prejudice against him, and the backwoods statesman was not willing to leave it unanswered. Gener-

ally he was quite well able to take care of himself, and did not fail in the present instance.

This is his reply :

" The Judge is wofully at fault about his early
friend Lincoln being a grocery-keeper. I don't
know as it would be a great sin if I had been ;
but he is mistaken. Lincoln never kept a grocery
anywhere in the world. It is true that Lincoln
did work the latter part of one winter in a little
still-house up at the head of a hollow. And so I
think my friend, the Judge, is equally at fault
when he charges me at the time when I was in
Congress with having opposed our soldiers who
were fighting in the Mexican war. The Judge
did not make his charge very distinctly, but I can
tell you what he can prove by referring to the
record. You remember I was an old Whig, and
whenever the Democratic party tried to get me to
vote that the war had been righteously begun by
the President, I would not do it. But whenever
they asked for any money, or land-warrants, or
anything to pay the soldiers there, during all that
time I gave the same vote that Judge Douglas did.
You can think as you please as to whether that was
consistent. Such is the truth ; and the Judge has a

right to make all he can out of it. But when he,
by a general charge, conveys the idea that I withheld supplies from the soldiers who were fighting
in the Mexican war, or did anything else to hin-
der the soldiers, he is, to say the least, grossly and
altogether mistaken, as a consultation of the rec-
ords will prove to him."

Not content with defending himself, Mr. Lincoln essayed on his side to contrast his opponent
and himself, and, like him, he indulged in personal reminiscences.

" 'Twenty-two years ago Judge Douglas and I
first became acquainted; we were both young
then —he a trifle younger than I. Even then we
were both ambitious,—I perhaps quite as much
so as he. With me the race of ambition has been
a failure,—a flat failure; with him it has been
one of splendid success. His name fills the nation, and is not unknown even in foreign lands.
I affect no contempt for the high eminence he
has reached,—so reached that the oppressed of
my species might have shared with me in the elevation. I would rather stand on that eminence
than wear the richest crown that ever pressed a
monarch's brow."

In another connection Mr. Lincoln says: " Senator Douglas is of world-wide renown. All the anxious politicians of his party, or who had been of his party for years past, have been looking upon him as certainly, at no distant day, to be the President of the United States. They have seen in his round, jolly, fruitful face, post-offices, land-offices, marshalships, and cabinet appointments, chargéships and foreign missions, bursting and sprouting out in wonderful exuberance, ready to be laid hold of by their greedy hands. And as they have been gazing upon this attractive picture so long, they can not, in the little distraction that has taken place in the party, bring themselves to give up the charming hope; but, with greedier anxiety, they rush about him, sustain him, and give him marches, triumphal entries, and receptions, beyond what, even in the days of his highest prosperity, they could have brought about in his favor. On the contrary, nobody has ever expected me to be President. In *my* poor, lean, lank face nobody has ever seen that any cabbages were sprouting out. There are disadvantages, all taken together, that the Republicans labor under. We have to fight this battle upon principle, and upon princip'e alone."

It may be said, in summing up, that Mr. Lincoln proved himself to be fully a match for Judge Douglas in this memorable campaign. I may go further and say that he overmatched him, for he adroitly propounded questions which his opponent was compelled to answer, and did answer in a way that killed him as a Presidential candidate. Though he ran in 1860, it was as an independent candidate. He had failed to retain the full confidence of his party, and could not secure the regular nomination. Indeed, he contributed indirectly to Lincoln's election, by dividing his own party, so that Mr. Lincoln became President, though receiving considerably less than one-half of the popular vote. It is obvious that Mr. Lincoln, who admits, as we have seen, that he was quite as ambitious as Douglas, was looking farther than the Senatorship. Yet he was personally disappointed when the majority in the Legislature proved to be for Douglas, and secured the election of the latter. He expressed this in his usual quaint way when some one asked him how he felt. He said, "that he felt like the boy that stubbed his toe,—it hurt too bad to laugh, and he was too big to cry."

It is probable that Abraham Lincoln, though he says no one had ever expected him to be President, was not without Presidential aspirations. He thought no doubt that an election as Senator would help his chances, and that the Senatorial position would prove a stepping-stone. Even the shrewdest, however, are liable to make mistakes, and we are led to believe that Mr. Lincoln was mistaken in this instance. If he had triumphed over Douglas in 1858, it is more than likely that by some word or act as Senator he would have aroused prejudices that would have made him unavailable in 1860, and the nation would never have discovered the leader who, under Providence, led it out of the wilderness, and conducted it to peace and freedom. I do not want to moralize overmuch, but can not help saying to my readers that in the lives of all there are present disappointments that lead to ultimate success and prosperity. It would not be hard to adduce convincing proofs. Washington and Garfield both desired to go to sea when they were boys. Had their wishes been gratified their after-careers might have been very different. Cromwell had made all arrangements to sail for America when still obscure. He was prevented, and remained in his own country to control its destiny, and take a position at the head of affairs. Remember this when your cherished plans are defeated. There is a higher wisdom than ours that shapes and directs our lives.

CHAPTER XVIII.

HENCEFORTH Abraham Lincoln was a marked man. He had sprung into national prominence. Limited as had been his tenure of office—including only two years in the lower house of Congress—it is remarkable how suddenly he came to be recognized as a leader. But at the East he was known only by reputation. This was soon remedied. He received an invitation to lecture in New York, or rather in Mr. Beecher's church in Brooklyn. He was well pleased to accept, but stipulated that he should be permitted to speak on a political subject. When he reached New York, he found that a change had been made in the place where he was to speak, and the Cooper Institute, where at intervals nearly every eminent man in the country has been heard, had been engaged for his début.

It was not without a feeling of modest shyness that he surveyed the immense audience gathered to hear him, and he was surprised to see the most cultivated citizens of the great metropolis upon the platform. Among them was William Cullen Bryant, who was president of the meeting, and in that capacity introduced him as "an eminent citizen of the West, hitherto known to you only by reputation."

Mr. Lincoln commenced his address in low tones, but his voice became louder and his manner more confident as he proceeded. His speech was an elaborate argument to prove that the original framers of the American Government intended that the Federal Government should exercise absolute control of the Federal territories, so far as the subject of slavery was concerned, and had never surrendered this high privilege to local legislation. This he established by incontrovertible proof, and in so doing quite upset Senator Douglas' theory of Squatter Sovereignty. Incidentally he vindicated the right of the Republican party to exist.

I have not room to quote from this remarkable speech. I am afraid I have already introduced

more extracts from speeches than my young readers will enjoy.   They are necessary, however, if
we would understand what were the views of
Mr. Lincoln, and what made him President.

The next day Mr. Lincoln's speech was printed
in full in two prominent papers—the *Tribune*
and the *Evening Post*, accompanied by'comments
of the most favorable character.   The first was
edited by Horace Greeley, the latter by the poet
Bryant, who was nearly as conspicuous a politician as a poet.   " No man ever before made such
an impression on his first appeal to a New York
audience," said the *Tribune.*

Robert Lincoln, Mr. Lincoln's oldest son, was
a student at Harvard, and his father travelled
into New England to visit him.   He was besieged
by applications to speak at Republican meetings,
and accepted a few invitations, being everywhere
cordially received.   This visit no doubt bore
fruit, and drew many voters to his standard, when
he had been formally presented to the country as
a candidate for the Presidency.   That my readers may learn how he spoke, and how he appeared, I quote from the Manchester (N. H.)
Mirror, an independent paper :

" He spoke an hour and a half with great fairness, great apparent candor, and with wonderful interest. He did not abuse the South, the administration, or the Democrats, or indulge in any personalities, with the exception of a few hits at Douglas' notions. He is far from prepossessing in personal appearance, and his voice is disagreeable; and yet he wins your attention and goodwill from the start. He indulges in no flowers of rhetoric, no eloquent passages. He is not a wit, a humorist, or a clown; yet so great a vein of pleasantry and good-nature pervades what he says, gilding over a deep current of practical argument he keeps his hearers in a smiling mood, with their mouths open ready to swallow all he says. His sense of the ludicrous is very keen; and an exhibition of that is the clincher of all his arguments,—not the ludicrous acts of persons, but ludicrous ideas. Hence he is never offensive, and steals away willingly into his train of belief persons who were opposed to him. For the first half hour his opponents would agree with everything he uttered; and from that point he began to lead them off little by little, until it seemed as if he had got them all into his fold. He displays more shrewdness, more knowledge of the masses of mankind, than any public speaker we have heard since Long Jim Wilson left for California."

On the day succeeding his speech in Norwich, he met in the cars a clergyman named Gulliver, who sought his acquaintance.

" Mr. Lincoln," he said, " I thought your speech last evening the most remarkable I ever heard."

" You do not mean this ? " said Mr. Lincoln, incredulously.

"Indeed, sir," said Gulliver, " I learned more of the art of public speaking last evening than I could from a whole course of lectures on rhetoric."

Mr. Lincoln was puzzled, for he was not a man to accept extravagant compliments.

" I should like very much to know what it was in my speech which you thought so remarkable," he said.

" The clearness of your statements," answered Gulliver, " the unanswerable style of your reasoning, and especially your illustrations, which were romance and pathos, and fun and logic, all welded together."

" I am much obliged to you for this," said Mr.

Lincoln. "I have been wishing for a long time to find some one who would make this analysis for me. It throws light on a subject which has been dark to me. I can understand very readily how such a power as you have ascribed to me will account for the effect which seems to be produced by my speeches. I hope you have not been too flattering in your estimate. Certainly I have had a most wonderful success for a man of my limited education."

"Mr. Lincoln, may I say one thing to you before we separate?" asked Mr. Gulliver later.

"Certainly; anything you please."

"You have spoken of the tendency of political life in Washington to debase the moral convictions of our representatives there, by the admixture of considerations of mere political expediency. You have become, by the controversy with Mr. Douglas, one of our leaders in this great struggle with slavery, which is undoubtedly *the* struggle of the nation and the age. What I would like to say is this, and I say it with a full heart: *Be true to your principles, and we will be true to you, and God will be true to us all!*"

"I say amen to that! amen to that!" answered

Mr. Lincoln, taking his hand in both his own, while his face lighted up sympathetically.

I may as well mention here the first public occasion on which Mr. Lincoln's name was mentioned for the Presidency.

On the 9th and 10th of May the Republican State Convention met at Decatur. Mr. Lincoln was present as a spectator, but he attracted the attention of Gov. Oglesby, who rose, and said: "I am informed that a distinguished citizen of Illinois, and one whom Illinois will ever delight to honor, is present; and I wish to move that this body invite him to a seat on the stand."

Public interest and curiosity were aroused. Who was this distinguished citizen?

The Governor paused a moment, and then uttered the name of Abraham Lincoln.

Instantly there was a roar of applause, there was a rush to where the astonished Lincoln sat, he was seized, and the crowd being too dense to press through, he was literally passed over the heads and shoulders of the great throng until breathless he found himself on the platform. Willing or unwilling he was literally for the time being "in the hands of his friends."

Later on Gov. Oglesby rose once more and said : "There is an old Democrat outside who has something which he wishes to present to the Convention."

"What is it ?" "What is it ?" "Receive it !" shouts the crowd.

The door of the wigwam opens, and an old man, bluff and hearty, comes forward, bearing on his shoulder two small rails, surmounted by a banner, with this inscription :—

TWO RAILS

From a lot made by Abraham Lincoln and John Hanks, in the Sangamon Bottom, in the year 1830.

This old man was John Hanks himself ! His entrance was greeted with tumultuous applause.

"Lincoln ! Lincoln ! A speech !" shouts the crowd.

Mr. Lincoln seemed amused. He rose at length and said :

"Gentlemen, I suppose you want to know something about those things," (the rails). " Well, the truth is, John Hanks and I did make rails in

the Sanganon Bottom. I don't know whether
we made those rails or not; fact is, I don't think
they are a credit to the makers," (laughing as he
spoke). "But I do know this: I made rails then,
and I think I could make better ones than these
now."

Before the Convention dissolved, a resolution
was passed, declaring that "Abraham Lincoln is
the first choice of the Republican party of Illinois for the Presidency, and instructing the dele-
gates to the Chicago Convention to use all honorable means to secure his nomination, and to cast
the vote of the State as a unit for him."

So Abraham Lincoln, "the rail-splitter," as he
was familiarly called, was fairly in the field as a
candidate for the highest office in the gift of the
nation.

CHAPTER XIX.

NOMINATED FOR PRESIDENT.

On the 16th of May the Republican Convention assembled in Chicago. Considered with
reference to its outcome, no more important convention had assembled since the organization of
the Government. Though this could not be realized at the time, its deliberations were followed
with great interest all over the country. The
opponents of the slave power were, for the first
time, to make a formidable effort to prevent its
extension and indefinite perpetuation.

Of course, there had been more or less election-
eering in advance. Half a dozen candidates were
in the field; but there were two who were recognized as leading in strength and popularity.
These were William H. Seward and Abraham
Lincoln. The former, in length and variety of
public service, in general culture, and national

reputation, was far superior. It was felt that he
would make an admirable candidate, and that he
deserved the nomination; but there were many
who were strongly opposed to him. Three important States—Pennsylvania, New Jersey, and
Indiana—declared that, as against Douglas, they
could do nothing if Seward were the nominee.
Illinois, of course, was for Lincoln, and this
giant of the Western prairies enjoyed a popularity which his more experienced competitor
could not boast. Yet for the first two days
Seward's chances seemed the better of the two.
The other candidates whose names were presented to the Convention were Mr. Dayton, of New
Jersey; Mr. Cameron, of Pennsylvania; Edward
Bates, of Missouri; and Ohio offered two distinguished sons—Salmon P. Chase and John
McLean.

On the first and second ballots Mr. Seward led;
but, on the third, Mr. Lincoln lacked but a vote
and a half of the number necessary to make him
the nominee. An Ohio delegate rose and changed
four votes from Chase to Lincoln. This was sufficient. He was nominated. The vast building
shook with the cheers of the dense throng. State

after State changed its vote to the man of destiny, and his nomination was made unanimous. In the afternoon, Hannibal Hamlin, of Maine, was nomi-nated for Vice-President.

Meanwhile Mr. Lincoln was in Springfield, bearing the suspense as well as he could. My boy readers will be interested to know that he spent a considerable part of his time in playing base-ball, his mind being too preoccupied to do his ordinary work. Dispatches were received from time to time, but nothing decisive.

Mr. Lincoln and some of his friends were wait-ing in the office of the *Journal* when the local editor rushed in, in a fever of excitement.

"What's the news?" was the breathless in-quiry.

"The Convention has made a nomination," he said, "and Mr. Seward——"

A look of intense disappointment was begin-ning to show itself on the faces of the listeners. They supposed that Seward was nominated.

"And Seward is—the second man on the list," continued the editor.

He could no longer restrain himself. Jumping on the editorial table, he shouted, "Gentlemen, I propose three cheers for Abraham Lincoln, the next President of the United States."

The cheers were given with a will.

The dispatch was handed to Mr. Lincoln, who read it quietly.

Then he put it in his pocket, saying, " There is a little woman on Eighth Street who will be interested to hear this," and he walked home.

In Springfield the news excited the greatest enthusiasm. All knew and loved Abraham Lincoln. He set himself above no one, but greeted all with cordial kindness. The nomination was felt to be a personal compliment to Springfield. The country had come to them for a President, and to the man above all others whom they would personally have selected.

That day Mr. Lincoln had to keep open house. His modest residence proved quite too small to contain the crowds who wanted to enter and shake hands with the man who had become so suddenly of national importance. They received a cordial welcome; and no one could detect in the nominee any unusual elation nor any deviation from his usual plain and modest deportment.

The next day Mr. Lincoln was formally notified of his election by a Committee of the Convention, with Mr. Ashmun at the head. This
was his response:

"MR. CHAIRMAN AND GENTLEMEN OF THE COM-
MITTEE:—I tender to you, and through you to
the Republican National Convention, and all the
people represented in it, my profoundest thanks
for the high honor done me, which you now formally announce. Deeply and even painfully
sensible of the great responsibility which is in-
separable from this high honor—a responsibility
which I could almost wish had fallen upon some
one of the far more eminent men and experienced statesmen whose distinguished names were
before the Convention, I shall, by your leave,
consider more fully the resolutions of the Convention, denominated the platform, and, without
unnecessary and unreasonable delay, respond to
you, Mr. Chairman, in writing, not doubting that
the platform will be found satisfactory, and the
nomination gratefully accepted. And now I will
not longer defer the pleasure of taking you, and
each of you, by the hand."

Let us consider who were Mr. Lincoln's rivals

in the Presidential race. Usually there are but two tickets in the field. This time there were four. First in order of time had come the National Constitutional Union Convention, made up largely of old Whigs. At this Convention John Bell, of Tennessee, was nominated for President, and Edward Everett, of Massachusetts, for Vice-President. The Democratic National Convention had met at Charleston, but adjourned without deciding upon a candidate. Mr. Douglas was the most prominent man before it, but extreme Southerners doubted his entire devotion to slavery, and he was unable to obtain the necessary two-thirds vote. The two factions into which the Convention split afterward met: the one at Baltimore, the other at Richmond. At the Baltimore Convention Stephen A. Douglas was nominated for President, and Mr. Johnson, of Georgia, for Vice-President. At the Richmond Convention of Southern seceders, John C. Breckinridge, of Kentucky, and Joseph Lane, of Oregon, were selected as standard-bearers.

In this division of the Democracy lay the hope of the new Republican party. With the Democracy united they would have been unable to

cope; but they were stronger than either faction.
When the eventful 6th of November arrived, the
result was what might have been anticipated.
Abraham Lincoln, the poor boy whose fortunes
we have so long followed, reached the highest step
of political preferment. He received 1,857,610
votes; Mr. Douglas came next, with 1,291,574;
while Mr. Breckinridge could muster only 850,082;
Mr. Bell secured 646,124. Of the electoral votes,
however, Mr. Lincoln received a majority, namely,
180 out of 292.

To go back a little. From the day of Mr. Lincoln's nomination he was beset by callers—some
drawn by curiosity, and many by considerations
of private interest. They found him the same
unaffected, plain man that he had always been.
He even answered the door-bell himself, and personally ushered visitors in and out. My readers
will be interested in two anecdotes of this time,
which I transcribe from the interesting volume
of Dr. Holland, already more than once referred to:

"Mr. Lincoln being seated in conversation with
a gentleman one day, two raw, plainly-dressed
young 'Suckers' entered the room and bashfully

lingered near the door. As soon as he observed them and apprehended their embarrassment, he rose and walked to them, saying, 'How do you do, my good fellows? What can I do for you? Will you sit down?'

"The spokesman of the pair, the shorter of the two, declined to sit, and explained the object of the call thus: he had had a talk about the relative height of Mr. Lincoln and his companion, and had asserted his belief that they were of exactly the same height. He had come in to verify his judgment. Mr. Lincoln smiled, went and got his cane, and, placing the end of it upon the wall, said, 'Here, young man, come under here.'

"The young man came under the cane, as Mr. Lincoln held it, and when it was perfectly adjusted to his height, Mr. Lincoln said, 'Now come out, and hold up the cane.' This he did, while Mr. Lincoln stepped under. Rubbing his head back and forth to see that it worked easily under the measurement, he stepped out, and declared to the sagacious fellow who was curiously looking on, that he had guessed with remarkable accuracy—that he and the young man were ex

actly of the same height. Then he shook hands
with them, and sent them on their way. Mr. Lincoln would just as soon have thought of cutting
off his right hand as he would have thought of
turning those boys away with the impression that
they had in any way insulted his dignity.

"They had hardly disappeared when an old
and modestly-dressed woman made her appearance. She knew Mr. Lincoln, but Mr Lincoln did
not at first recognize her. Then she undertook
to recall to his memory certain incidents connected with his ride upon the Circuit—especially
upon his dining at her house upon the road at different times. Then he remembered her and her
home. Having fixed her own place in her recol-
lection, she tried to recall to him a certain scanty
dinner of bread and milk that he once ate at her
house. He could not remember it; on the contrary, he only remembered that he had always
fared well at her house. 'Well,' said she, 'one
day you came along after we had got through
dinner, and we had eaten up everything, and I
could give you nothing but a bowl of bread and
milk; and you ate it; and when you got up you
said it was good enough for the President of the

United States.' The good old woman, remembering the remark, had come in from the country,
making a journey of eight or ten miles, to relate
to Mr. Lincoln this incident, which, in her mind,
had doubtless taken the form of prophecy. Mr.
Lincoln placed the honest creature at her ease,
chatted with her of old' times, and dismissed her
in the most happy and complacent frame of
mind."

CHAPTER XX.

HOWEVER bitter and acrimonious a political campaign may have been, the result is usually accepted good-naturedly. The defeated party hopes for better luck next time, and awaits with interest the course of the new Executive. But this was not the case after the election which made Mr. Lincoln President. The South was sullen, the North divided in sentiment. The party that sustained slavery had staked all on the issue of the campaign. They were not disposed to acquiesce in the result. They were quiet, but it was a dangerous quiet. They were biding their time, and meant mischief.

James Buchanan was President. He was an old man; cautious to timidity, overawed by the bold, defiant spirits that constituted his Cabinet— not seeing, or not caring to see, the evidences of

(183)

their disloyalty.   Never did a President long more ardently for his term to close.   He saw that a storm was brewing, the like of which the country had never seen.   He earnestly hoped that it would not burst till he had laid down the responsibilities of office.

Abraham Lincoln waited quietly at Springfield for the time to come that should separate him from the tranquil course of life he had led hitherto and precipitate him into the maelstrom of political excitement at Washington, wherein he was to be the central figure.   Knowing him as in after years we learned to know him, we can not doubt that at times he felt almost overwhelmed by his coming burdens.   It was well, perhaps, that he was not permitted to be too much alone.   His attention was distracted by throngs of visitors, —autograph-hunters and office-seekers being the most conspicuous—who consumed a large part of his time.

As this story is written especially for young people, I will venture to transcribe from Mr. Holland's " Life " two incidents which connected him with children :

" He was holding a reception at the Tremont

House in Chicago. A fond father took in a little boy by the hand who was anxious to see the new President. The moment the child entered the parlor door, he of his own motion, and quite to the surprise of his father, took off his hat, and, giving it a swing, cried, ' Hurrah for Lincoln ! ' There was a crowd, but as soon as Mr. Lincoln could get hold of the little fellow, he lifted him in his hands, and, tossing him toward the ceiling, laughingly shouted, ' Hurrah for you ! '

" To Mr. Lincoln it was evidently a refreshing episode in the dreary work of hand-shaking.

" At a party in Chicago during this visit, he saw a little girl timidly approaching him. He called her to him, and asked her what she wished for. She replied that she wanted his name. Mr. Lincoln looked back into the room, and said, ' But here are other little girls—they would feel badly if I should give my name only to you.' The little girl replied that there were eight in all. ' Then,' said Mr. Lincoln, ' get me eight sheets of paper and pen and ink and I will see what I can do for you.' The paper was brought, and Mr. Lincoln sat down in the crowded drawing-room, and wrote a sentence upon each sheet, appending his name; and thus every little girl carried off her souvenir."

On the 11th of February, 1861, Abraham Lincoln left his pleasant Western home for the capital. It was to be a leisurely journey, for he would be expected to stop at many points to meet friends and receive friendly greetings. Three weeks were to elapse before he would be inaugurated, but, as he bade farewell to his friends and neighbors, he felt that the burden of care had already fallen upon him. How he felt may be understood from the few farewell words which he spoke. As reported by Mr. Lamon, they are as follows:

"FRIENDS :—No one who has never been placed in a like position can understand my feelings at this hour, nor the oppressive sadness I feel at this parting. For more than a quarter of a century I have lived among you, and, during all that time, I have received nothing but kindness at your hands. Here I have lived from my youth, until now I am an old man. Here the most sacred ties of earth were assumed. Here all my children were born, and here one of them lies buried. To you, dear friends, I owe all that I have—all that I am. All the strange, checkered past seems to crowd upon my mind. To-day I leave you. I go to assume a task more difficult than that which devolved upon Washington. Unless the great God who assisted him shall be with and aid me, I must fail; but, if the same Omniscient mind and almighty arm that directed and protected him shall guide and support me, I shall not fail—I shall succeed. Let us all pray that the God of our fathers may not forsake us now. To Him I commend you all. Permit me to ask that, with equal security and faith, you will invoke His wisdom and guidance for me. With these few words, I must leave you; for how long, I know not. Friends, one and all, I must now bid you an affectionate farewell."

I have already alluded to Mr. Lincoln's constitutional melancholy inherited from his mother. With it was joined a vein of superstition, which at times darkened the shadow that seemed to hover about him. In this connection, and as an illustration of this characteristic of the President-elect, I quote an interesting reminiscence of John Hay, the secretary of Mr. Lincoln, in the words of his chief:

"It was just after my election in 1860, when the news had been coming in thick and fast all day, and there had been a great 'hurrah, boys!' so that I was well tired out, and went home to rest, throwing myself upon a lounge in my chamber. Opposite to where I lay was a bureau with a swinging glass upon it; and, in looking in that glass, I saw myself reflected nearly at full length; but my face, I noticed, had two separate and distinct images—the tip of the nose of one being about three inches from the tip of the other. I was a little bothered—perhaps startled, and got up and looked in the glass, but the illusion vanished. On lying down again I saw it a second time—plainer, if possible, than before; and then I noticed that one of the faces was a little paler—say, five shades—than the other. I got up, and the thing melted away; and I went off, and in the excitement of the hour forgot all about it—nearly, but not quite; for the thing would once in a while come up and give me a little pang, as if something uncomfortable had happened. When I went home, I told my wife about it; and a few days after, I tried the experiment again—when, sure enough, the thing came back again; but I never succeeded in bringing back the ghost after that, though I once tried very industriously to show it to my wife, who was worried about it somewhat. She thought it was a 'sign' that I was to be elected to a second term of office, and that the paleness of one of the faces was an omen that I should not see life through the last term."

Mrs. Lincoln's impression was curiously correct, as it turned out; but we must set it down as a singular coincidence, and nothing more. Campbell, in one of his spirited lyrics, tells us that "Coming events cast their shadows before"; but it is hardly likely that in this case God should have sent the President-elect a premonition of the fate which was to overtake him some years later. It is better to consider that the vision had a natural cause in the rumors of assassination which were even then rife on account of the bitter feeling excited by the election of a Republican President. Such rumors had been brought to Mr. Lincoln himself, and he had been urged to take measures against assassination. But he considered them useless. "If they want to kill me," he said, "there is nothing to prevent." He felt that it would be easy enough for an enemy to take his life, no matter how many guards he might have around him. If it were his destiny to die, he felt that death would come in spite of all precautions.

I need hardly say that Mr. Lincoln was unfortunate in having such a temperament. Fortunately, it is exceptional. A cheerful, sunny temperament, that rejoices in prosperity and makes the best of adversity, providing against ill-fortune, but not anticipating it, is a happy possession. In Mr. Lincoln his morbid feelings were lighted up and relieved by a strong sense of humor, which made him in his lighter moments a very agreeable companion.

CHAPTER XXI.

BEFORE proceeding to speak of Abraham Lincoln as President, I desire that my readers may know him as well as possible, and for that purpose I will transcribe an account of a visit to him by a correspondent of the New York *Evening Post.* I find it in D. W. Bartlett's book, entitled " The Life and Public Services of Hon. Abraham Lincoln ":

" It had been reported by some of Mr. Lincoln's political enemies that he was a man who lived in the lowest Hoosier style, and I thought I would see for myself. Accordingly, as soon as the business of the Convention was closed, 1 took the cars for Springfield. I found Mr. Lincoln living in a handsome, but not pretentious, double two-story frame house, having a wide hall running through the center, with parlors on both sides, neatly, but

(191)

not ostentatiously furnished. It was just such a dwelling as a majority of the well-to-do residents of these fine Western towns occupy. Everything about it had a look of comfort and independence. The library I remarked in passing particularly, and I was pleased to see long rows of books, which told of the scholarly tastes and culture of the family.

" Lincoln received us with great, and, to me, surprising, urbanity. I had seen hin before in New York, and brought with me an impression of his awkward and ungainly manner; but in his own house, where he doubtless feels himself freer than in the strange New York circles, he had thrown this off, and appeared easy if not graceful.

" He is, as you know, a tall, lank man, with a long neck, and his ordinary movements are unusually angular, even out West. As soon, however, as he gets interested in conversation, his face lights up, and his attitudes and gestures assume a certain dignity and impressiveness. His conversation is fluent, agreeable, and polite. You see at once from it that he is a man of decided and original character. His views are all his own; such as he has worked out from a patient and va-

ried scrutiny of life, and not such as he has learned from others. Yet he can not be called opin-
ionated. He listens to others like one eager to
learn, and his replies evince at the same time both
modesty and self-reliance. I should say that
sound common-sense was the principal quality of
his mind, although at times a striking phrase or
word reveals a peculiar vein of thought. He tells
a story well, with a strong idiomatic smack, and
seems to relish humor, both in himself and others.
Our conversation was mainly political, but of a
general nature. One thing Mr. Lincoln remarked which I will venture to repeat. He said that
in the coming Presidential canvass he was wholly
uncommitted to any cabals or cliques, and that he
meant to keep himself free from them, and from
all pledges and promises.

"I had the pleasure also of a brief interview
with Mrs. Lincoln, and, in the circumstances of
these persons, I trust I am not trespassing on the
sanctities of private life, in saying a word in regard to that lady. Whatever of awkwardness
may be ascribed to her husband, there is none of
it in her. On the contrary, she is quite a pattern
of ladylike courtesy and polish. She converses

with freedom and grace, and is thoroughly *au fait* in all the little amenities of society. Mrs. Lincoln belongs, by the mother's side, to the Preston family of Kentucky ; has received a liberal and refined education, and, should she ever reach it, will adorn the White House. She is, I am told, a strict and consistent member of the Presbyterian church.

"Not a man of us who saw Mr. Lincoln but was impressed by his ability and character. In illustration of the last, let me mention one or two things which your readers, I think, will be pleased to hear. Mr. Lincoln's early life, as you know, was passed in the roughest kind of experience on the frontier, and among the roughest sort of people. Yet, I have been told, that, in the face of all these influences, he is a strictly temperate man, never using wine or strong drink, and, stranger still, he does not 'twist the filthy weed,' nor smoke, nor use profane language of any kind. When we consider how common these vices are all over our country, particularly in the West, it must be admitted that it exhibits no little strength of character to have refrained from them.

"Mr. Lincoln is popular with his friends and

neighbors; the habit ial equity of his mind points
him out as a peace-maker and composer of difficulties; his integrity is proverbial; and his legal
abilities are regarded as of the highest order.
The *sobriquet* of 'Honest Old Abe' has been won
by years of upright conduct, and is the popular
homage to his probity. He carries the marks of
honesty in his face and entire deportment.

"I am the more convinced by this personal in-
tercourse with Mr. Lincoln, that the action of our
Convention was altogether judicious and proper."

I call the attention of my readers to what is
said of Mr. Lincoln's freedom from bad habits of
every kind, though brought up as he had been,
and with the surroundings of his early life, it
would have been natural for him to fall into them.

During Mr. Lincoln's visit to New York, he
visited the Five Points House of Industry. This
was probably at the time of his first visit, already
referred to. when he made an address at the
Cooper Institute. One who was at that time a
teacher in the House of Industry, gives this account of the visit:

"Our Sunday-school in the Five Points was assembled one Sabbath morning, a few months

since, when I noticed a tall and remarkable-look-
ing man enter the room and take a seat among us.
He listened with fixed attention to our exercises,
and his countenance manifested such genuine interest that I approached him and suggested that
he might be willing to say something to the children.

"He accepted the invitation with evident
pleasure, and, coming forward, began a simple address, which at once fascinated every little hearer,
and hushed the room into silence. His language
was strikingly beautiful, and his tones musical
with intensest feeling. The little faces around
would droop into sad conviction as he uttered
sentences of warning, and would brighten into
sunshine as he spoke cheerful words of promise.
Once or twice he attempted to close his remarks,
but the imperative shouts of 'Go on!' 'Oh, do
go on!' would compel him to resume. As I
looked upon the gaunt and sinewy frame of the
stranger, and marked his powerful head and determined features, now touched into softness by
the impressions of the moment, I felt an irrepressible curiosity to learn something more about
him, and when he was quietly leaving the room,

I begged to know his name. He courteously replied:

"'It is Abraham Lincoln, from Illinois!'"

It is easy to understand how the sight of these
poor children should have touched the heart of
the backwoods boy. Doubtless they recalled to
his memory his own neglected childhood, and his
early privations, when he was not in a position to
learn even as well as these poor waifs from the
city streets. If only that speech could have been
reported, with what interest would we read it to-
day. It must have been instinct with sympathy
to have made such a powerful impression on these
poor children and the teacher who tells the story.

CHAPTER XXII

THERE were unusual circumstances attending the close of Mr. Lincoln's journey to the Capital. So bitter was the feeling engendered among his opponents that plots were entered into against his life. Dr. Holland states that the President-elect was cognizant of his danger. An attempt was made to throw the train off the track on which he journeyed from Springfield. There was a rumor that when he reached Baltimore conspirators would surround his carriage in the guise of friends, and accomplish his assassination. These reports were probably exaggerated, and Mr. Lamon discredits them altogether, but it is likely that they were well founded. At any rate, measures were taken to ferret out the conspiracy, and, by advice of General Scott and Senator Seward, then in Washington, Mr. Lincoln quietly left

(198)

Harrisburg by a special train in advance of his party, and arrived in Washington at half-past six in the morning, when no one expected him except those who had arranged this deviation from the regular programme. The moment he left Harrisburg the telegraph wires were cut, so that intelligence of his departure could not be sent to a distance.

It was strange and as yet unprecedented, this secret and carefully-guarded journey, but the circumstances seemed to make it necessary. His friends received him with a feeling of happy relief, and, as the morning advanced, and it was learned that he was in the city, Washington enjoyed a sensation. There were many at the time who ridiculed the fears of Mr. Lincoln's friends, and disapproved of the caution which counselled his secret arrival; but sad events that have since saddened and disgraced the nation, show that both he and his friends were wise. The assassination of Lincoln on his way to the Capital would have had far more disastrous effects than the unhappy tragedy of April, 1865, and might have established Jefferson Davis in the White House.

There was a strong disloyal element in Washington, and there were more perhaps who regarded Mr. Lincoln with hostility than with friendship, but among those who probably were heartily glad to hear of his arrival was President James Buchanan, who was anxious and eager to lay down the sceptre, and transfer his high office to his lawful successor. Timid by nature, he was not the pilot to guide the ship of State in a storm. No one ever more willingly retired to the peace and security of private life.

Indeed, as we consider the condition of the country and the state of public feeling, we are disposed rather to condole with the new President than to congratulate him. In times of peace and prosperity the position of Chief Magistrate is a prize worth competing for ; but, in 1861, even a strong man and experienced statesman might well have shrunk from assuming its duties.

General Winfield Scott was at that time in military command of Washington. He was fearful that the inaugural exercises might be interrupted by some violent demonstration, and made preparations accordingly, but he was happily disappointed. The day dawned bright and clear. Washington was in holiday attire. Business was

generaɪ y suspended, and there was au unusual in
terest to hear Mr. Lincoln's inaugural address.
Among the attentive listeners were the retiring
President and Chief-Justice Taney, of the Supreme Court, a man whose sympathies were with
the slave power. It was a creditable and noteworthy incident of this memorable occasion, that
among the friends who stood by Mr. Lincoln most
staunchly, even holding his hat as he delivered his
inaugural, was his old Senatorial and Presidential
competitor, Stephen A. Douglas. Whatever his
sentiments were on the issues of the day, he was
not willing to side with, or in any way assist,
those who menaced the national existence. Another defeated candidate, Mr. Breckinridge, was
present, having just surrendered the Vice-President's chair to Mr. Hamlin. It was a scene for
an artist. There could be no more striking picture than one which should faithfully represent
Abraham Lincoln, reading his first inaugural before an audience of representative men, half of
whom were hostile, and many of whom, three
months later, were in arms against the Government. All alike, foes as well as friends, were
eager to hear what the new President had to say

Had it been Seward instead of Lincoln, they could have formed a reasonable conjecture, but this giant from the Western prairies; this Backwoods Boy, who had grown to maturity under the most unpromising circumstances; this man, with his limited experience in but one national office, was an unknown quantity in politics, and no one knew what manner of man he was. But we shall never have such a picture. People had more important things to think of then, and it is too late now. In a time of intense feeling, when the national existence was at stake, and no one knew what events the next week would bring forth, there was little taste or time for art.

We, too, may well feel interested in the utterances of the President-elect. I should be glad to quote the entire address, but as this is impracticable, I will make a few significant extracts:

"I do not consider it necessary at present, said Mr. Lincoln, "for me to discuss those matters of administration about which there is no special anxiety or excitement. Apprehensions seem to exist among the people of the Southern States, that, by the accession of a Republican administration, their property and their peace and personal security are to be endangered. There has never been any reasonable cause for such apprehension. Indeed, the most ample evidence to the contrary has all the while existed, and been open to their inspection. It is found in nearly all the published speeches of him who now addresses you. I do but quote from one of those speeches, when I declare that 'I have no purpose, directly or indirectly, to interfere with the institution of slavery in the States where it exists.' I believe I have no lawful right to do so; and I have no inclination to do so. Those who nominated and elected me did so with the full knowledge that I had made this, and made many similar declarations, and had never recanted them."

Further on he says:

" It is seventy-two years to-day since the first inauguration of a President under our national Constitution. During that period fifteen different and very distinguished citizens have, in succession, administered the executive branch of the Government. They have conducted it through many perils, and generally with great success. Yet, with all this scope for precedent, I now enter upon the same task, for the brief constitutional term of four years, under great and peculiar difficulties.

" A disruption of the Federal Union, heretofore only menaced, is now formidably attempted. I hold that in the contemplation of, universal law and of the Constitution, the union of these States is perpetual. Perpetuity is implied, if not expressed, in the fundamental law of all national governments. It is safe to assert that no government proper ever had a provision in its organic law for its own termination. Continue to execute all the express provisions of our national Constitution, and the Union will endure forever, it being impossible to destroy it except by some action not provided for in the instrument itself.

" It follows from these views that no State, upon its own mere motion, can lawfully get out of the Union ; that resolves and ordinances to that effect are legally void ; and that acts of violence within any State or States against the authority of the United States are insurrectionary or revolutionary, according to circumstances.

" I therefore consider that, in view of the Constitution and the laws, the Union is unbroken, and, to the extent of my ability, I shall take care, as the Constitution itself expressly enjoins upon me, that the laws of the Union shall be faithfully executed in all the States. Doing this, which I deem to be only a simple duty on my part, I shall perfectly perform it, so far as is practicable, unless my rightful masters, the American people, shall withhold the requisition, or in some authoritative manner direct the contrary.

" I trust this will not be regarded as a menace, but only as the declared purpose of the Union, that it will constitutionally defend and maintain itself."

After arguing at some length against separation, Mr. Lincoln closes his address with an appeal to his fellow-citizens:

" My countrymen, one and all, think calmly and well upon this whole subject. Nothing valuable can be lost by taking time.

" If there be an object to hurry any of you, in hot haste, to a step which you would never take deliberately, that object will be frustrated by taking time; but no good object can be frustrated by it.

" Such of you as are now dissatisfied still have

the old Constitution unimpaired, and, on the sensitive point, the laws of your own framing, under it ; while the new administration will have no immediate power, if it would, to change either.

"If it were admitted that you who are dissatisfied hold the right side in the dispute, there is still no single reason for precipitate action. Intelligence, patriotism, Christianity, and a firm reliance on Him who has never yet forsaken this favored land, are still competent to adjust, in the best way, all our present difficulties.

"In your hands, my dissatisfied fellow-countrymen, and not in mine, is the momentous issue of civil war. The Government will not assail you.

"You can have no conflict without being yourselves the aggressors. You have no oath registered in heaven to destroy the Government, while I shall have the most solemn one to 'preserve, protect, and defend' it.

"I am loth to close. We are not enemies, but friends. We must not be enemies. Though passion may have strained, it must not break our bonds of affection.

"The mystic chords of memory, stretching from

every battle-field and patriotic grave to every living heart and hearthstone all over this broad land, will yet swell the chorus of the Union, when again touched, as surely they will be, by the better angels of our nature."

CHAPTER XXIII.

THE WAR BEGINS.

No President ever assumed office under such circumstances as Abraham Lincoln. Nominally chief magistrate of the whole United States, seven members of the confederation had already seceded. These were South Carolina, Georgia, Alabama, Mississippi, Texas, Florida, and Louisiana. Some had been hurried out of the Union by a few hot-headed politicians, against the wishes of a considerable part of their inhabitants. It is known that General Lee and Alexander H. Stephens, though they ultimately went with their States, were exceedingly reluctant to array themselves in opposition to the Government.

Mr. Stephens used these patriotic words in an address before the Legislature of Georgia, Nov. 14, 1860, after the result of the election was made known : " The first question that presents itself is, shall the people of the South secede from the Union in consequence of the election of Mr. Lincoln to the Presidency of the United States? My countrymen, I tell you candidly, frankly, and earnestly that I do not think that they ought. In my judgment the election of no man, constitutionally chosen to that high office, is sufficient cause for any State to separate from the Union. It ought to stand by and aid still in maintaining the Constitution of the country. To make a point of resistance to the Government, to withdraw from it because a man has been constitutionally elected, puts us in the wrong. . . . . We went into the election with this people. The result was different from what we wished; but the election has been constitutionally held. Were we to make a point of resistance to the Government, and go out of the Union on this account, the record would be made up hereafter against us."

*These wise and moderate counsels did not prevail. There was a feeling of bitterness which impelled Southern men to extreme measures. Moreover, the temper and firmness of the North were misunderstood. It was thought they would make the most humiliating concessions to preserve the integrity of the Union, while on the other hand the constancy and determination of the Southern people were not sufficiently appreciated at the North.

. Mr. Lincoln's first necessary act was to make choice of a Cabinet. He demonstrated his sagacity in surrounding himself with trained and experienced statesmen, as will be seen at once by the following list:

Secretary of State, William H. Seward, of New York; Secretary of the Treasury, Salmon P. Chase, of Ohio; Secretary of War, Simon Cameron, of Pennsylvania; Secretary of the Navy, Gideon Welles, of Connecticut; Secretary of the Interior, Caleb B. Smith, of Indiana; Postmaster-General, Montgomery Blair, of Maryland; Attorney-General, Edward Bates, of Missouri.

These gentlemen were confirmed, and entered upon the discharge of their duties. Thus the new Administration was complete. Simon Cameron, as Secretary of War, was superseded in less than a year by Edwin M. Stanton, who proved to be the right man in the right place. A man of remarkable executive talent, never shrinking from the heavy burden of labor and care which his office imposed, he worked indefatigably, and though he may have offended some by his brusque manners, and unnecessary sternness, it is doubtful whether a better man could have been selected for his post. He had been a member of Mr. Buchanan's Cabinet in its last days, and did what he could to infuse something of his own vigor into the timid and vacillating Executive.

It will be seen that Mr. Lincoln called to the most important place in the Cabinet the man who was his most prominent rival for the nomination, William H. Seward. In doing this he strengthened his administration largely in the minds of the people at large, for who was there who was ignorant of Mr. Seward's great ability and statesmanship? It may be remarked here that the new President left to each of his Secretaries large discretion in their respective departments, and did not interfere with or overrule them except in cases of extreme necessity. A man of smaller nature would have gratified his vanity and sense of importance by meddling with, and so marring the work of his constitutional advisers; but having selected the best men he could find, Mr. Lincoln left them free to act, and held them respon-

sible for the successful management of their de
partments.

The new President was not long left in uncer-
tainty as to the intentions of the seceding States.
On the 13th of March he received a communica-
tion from two gentlemen, claiming to be com-
missioners from a government composed of the
seven seceding States, expressing a desire to enter
upon negotiations for the adjustment of all questions growing out of the separation. To have received them would have been to admit the fact
and right of secession, and therefore their request
was denied. On the 11th of April, General
Beauregard, in accordance with instructions from
the rebel Secretary of War, demanded of Major
Anderson, in command at Fort Sumter, the surrender of the fort. Major Anderson declined,
but was compelled to do so on the morning of the
4th, after a bombardment of thirty-three hours.
Thus the South had taken the initiative, and had
made an armed attack upon the Government.
Thus far the President had pursued a conciliatory
—some thought it a timid—policy, but when he
heard that Sumter had been taken forcible
possession of by rebellious citizens, he felt that

there was no more room for hesitation. The time had come to act.

On the day succeeding the evacuation of the fort, he issued a proclamation calling for 75,000 soldiers to recover possession of the "forts, places, and property which have been seized from the Union," and at the same time summoned an extra session of both Houses of Congress, to assemble on Thursday, the fourth day of July, "to consider and determine such measures as, in their wisdom, the public safety and interest may seem to demand."

It is needless to say that the evacuation of Fort Sumter, and the President's proclamation, created a whirlwind of excitement. The South was jubilant, the North was deeply stirred, and the proclamation was generally approved and promptly responded to. These spirited lines of the poet Whittier are well called

THE VOICE OF THE NORTH.

Up the hill-side, down the glen
Rouse the sleeping citizen;
Summon out the might of men!

Like a lion growling low—
Like a night-storm rising slow—
Like the tread of unseen foe—

It is coming—it is nigh!
Stand your homes and altars by,
On your own free threshold die!

Clang the bells in all your spires,
On the grey hills of your sires
Fling to heaven your signal fires!

Oh! for God and duty stand,
Heart to heart, and hand to hand,
Round the old graves of the land.

Who so shrinks or falters now,
Who so to the yoke would bow,
Brand the craven on his brow.

Freedom's soil has only place
For a free and fearless race—
None for traitors false and base.

Perish party—perish clan,
Strike together while you can,
Like the strong arm of one man.

Like the angel's voice sublime,
Heard above a world of crime,
Crying for the end of Time.

With one heart and with one mouth
Let the North speak to the South;
Speak the word befitting both.

In contrast with this, I will cite a poem, which
might be called, not inappropriately,

THE VOICE OF THE SOUTH.

Rebels! 'tis a holy name !
  The name our fathers bore,
When battling in the cause of Right
Against the tyrant in his might,
  In the dark days of yore.

Rebels! 'tis our family name!
  Our father, Washington,
Was the arch rebel in the fight,
And gave the name to us—aright
  Of father unto son.

Rebels! 'tis our given name!
  Our mother Liberty
Received the title with her fame,
In days of grief, of fear and shame,
  When at her breast were we.

Rebels! 'tis our sealed name!
  ·A baptism of blood !
The war—ay, and the din of strife—
The fearful contest, life for life—
  The mingled crimson flood !

Rebels! 'tis a patriot's name !
  In struggles it was given ;
We bore it then when tyrants raved,
And through their curses 'twas engraved
  On the doomsday book of heaven.

Rebels! 'tis our fighting name!
  For peace rules o'er the land,

Until they speak of craven woe—
Until our rights received a blow,
From foes' or brother's hand.

Rebels! 'tis our dying name!
For although life is dear,
Yet freemen born and freemen bred,
We'd rather live as freemen dead
Than live in slavish fear.

Then call us Rebels if you will—
We glory in the name;
For bending under unjust laws,
And swearing faith to an unjust cause,
We count a greater shame.

CHAPTER XXIV.

AND thus commenced the great war of the Rebellion—a war which in some respects has never had its parallel. Commencing but a few weeks after Mr. Lincoln's administration began, it was at its last gasp when upon the 4th of March, 1865, he was for the second time inaugurated.

If I were to write a full account of Mr. Lincoln's administration, it must include a history of the war. I propose to do neither. As my title imports, I have aimed only to show by what steps a backwoods boy, born and brought up on the Western prairies, with the smallest possible advantages of education and fortune, came to stand in the foremost place among his fellow-citizens. I might, therefore, consider my task accomplished; but, if I should stop here, I should have failed to set forth fully the charac-

(217)

ter and traits of this remarkable man ; for it was only in the years of his Presidency that the world, and, I may add, his friends, came to know him as he was. I doubt even if he knew himself until the responsibilities of office fell upon him ; and, under the burden, he expanded to the full stature of a providential man. There are some aspects in which I shall consider him, and, in the incidents and anecdotes I may have to relate, I shall not attempt to preserve the order of time.

First, then, the consciousness of official rank never appeared present to Mr. Lincoln. In the White House, as in his modest Western home, he was the same plain, unpretending Abraham Lincoln. Nor did he lose his sympathy for the humble class from which he had himself sprung. Upon this point I quote from Mr. F. B. Carpenter's very interesting volume, already referred to :

"The Hon. Mr. Odell gave me a deeply interesting incident which occurred in the winter of 1864 at one of the most crowded of the Presidential levees, illustrating very perfectly Mr. Lincoln's true politeness and delicacy of feeling.

"On the occasion referred to the pressure became so great that the usual ceremony of hand-

shaking was for once discontinued. The President had been standing for some time, bowing
his acknowledgments to the thronging multitude, when his eye fell upon a couple who had
entered unobserved—a wounded soldier and his
plainly-dressed mother. Before they could pass
out he made his way to where they stood, and,
taking each of them by the hand, with a delicacy
and cordiality which brought tears to many eyes,
he assured them of his interest and welcome.
Governors, Senators, and diplomats passed with
simply a nod; but that pale, young face he
might never see again. To him and to others
like him did the nation owe his life; and Abraham Lincoln was not the man to forget this, even
in the crowded and brilliant assembly of the distinguished of the land."

"Mr. Lincoln's heart was always open to children," says the same writer. "I shall never forget his coming into the studio one day and finding my own little boy of two summers playing
on the floor. A member of the Cabinet was with
him, but, laying aside all restraint, he took the
little fellow at once in his arms, and they were
soon on the best of terms.

"Old Daniel gave me a touching illustration of this element in his character. A poor woman from Philadelphia had been waiting with a baby in her arms for several days to see the President. It appeared by her story that her husband had furnished a substitute for the army, but some time afterward, in a state of intoxication, was induced to enlist. When reaching the post assigned his regiment he deserted, thinking the Government was not entitled to his services. Returning home he was arrested, tried, convicted, and sentenced to be shot. The sentence was to be executed on a Saturday. On Monday his wife left her home with her baby to endeavor to see the President.

"Said Daniel, 'She had been waiting here three days, and there was no chance for her to get in. Late in the afternoon of the third day, the President was going through the passage to his private room to get a cup of tea. On the way he heard the baby cry. He instantly went back to his office and rang the bell.

"'"Daniel," said he, "is there a woman with a baby in the anteroom?"

"'I said there was, and if he would allow me

to say it, it was a case he ought to see; for it was a matter of life and death.

" ' " Send her to me at once," said he.

" ' She went in, told her story, and the President pardoned her husband. As the woman came out from his presence her eyes were lifted and her lips moving in prayer, the tears streaming down her cheeks.' Said Daniel, 'I went up to her, and, pulling her shawl, said, "Madam, it was the baby that did it." ' "

It may readily be supposed that a man of Mr. Lincoln's democratic tastes and training might on some occasions act very unconventionally, and in a way to shock those who are sticklers for etiquette. Certainly, he was very far from aping royalty, as may be judged from the following incident:

When the Prince of Wales was betrothed to the Princess Alexandra, Queen Victoria announced the fact to each of the European sovereigns and to the rulers of other countries by an autograph letter. Lord Lyons, the British ambassador at Washington, who was a bachelor, called upon President Lincoln to present this important document in person.

"May it please your Excellency," said the ambassador, with formal dignity, "I hold in my hand an autograph letter from my royal mistress, Queen Victoria, which I have been commanded to present to your Excellency. In it she informs your Excellency that her son, His Royal Highness, the Prince of Wales, is about to contract a matrimonial alliance with Her Royal Highness, the Princess Alexandra, of Denmark."

The President's eye twinkled as he answered, briefly, "Lord Lyons, go thou and do likewise."

Says Dr. Holland: "Mr. Lincoln's habits at the White House were as simple as they were at his old home in Illinois. He never alluded to himself as 'President,' or as occupying 'the Presidency.' His office he always designated as 'this place.' 'Call me Lincoln,' said he to a friend. 'Mr. President' had become so very tiresome to him. 'If you see a newsboy down the street, send him up this way,' said he to a passenger as he stood waiting for the morning news at his gate.

"Friends cautioned him against exposing himself so openly in the midst of enemies, but he never heeded them. He frequently walked the streets at night entirely unprotected, and he felt any check upon his free movements as a great annoyance. He delighted to see his familiar Western friends, and he gave them always a cordial welcome. He met them on the old footing, and fell at once into the accustomed habits of talking and story-telling. An old acquaintance with his wife visited Washington. Mr. and Mrs. Lincoln proposed to these friends a ride in the Presidential carriage. It should be stated in advance that the two men had probably never seen each other with gloves on in their lives, unless when they were used as protection from the cold. The question of each —Mr. Lincoln at the White House and his friend at the hotel—was whether he should wear gloves. Of course, the ladies urged gloves; but Mr. Lincoln only put his in his pocket, to be used or not, according to circumstances.

"When the Presidential party arrived at the hotel to take in their friends, they found the gentleman, overcome by his wife's persuasions, very handsomely gloved. The moment he took his seat he began to draw off the clinging kids, while Mr. Lincoln began to draw his on.

"'No, no, no!' protested his friend, tugging

at his gloves; 'it is none of my doings. Put up your gloves, Mr. Lincoln.'

"So the two old friends were on even and easy terms, and had their ride after their old fashion."

The President of the United States can afford to be more unconventional than kings and emperors, but I should not be surprised to learn that they too, at times, would be glad to escape from the rigid rules of etiquette and enjoy the freedom of a private citizen. Even Queen Victoria, it is related, can unbend when she meets her early friends, and forget for the time that she must maintain the dignity of a Queen.

CHAPTER XXV.

Ex-Governor Rice, of Massachusetts, tells a
story of President Lincoln, which will prove of
especial interest to my young readers. I transcribe it from the *Union Signal:*

On an occasion (while he was in Congress) he
and Senator Wilson found it necessary to visit
the President on business, he says:

" We were obliged to wait some time in the
anteroom before we could be received; and, when
at length the door was opened to us, a small lad,
perhaps ten or twelve years old, who had been
waiting for admission several days without success, slipped in between us, and approached the
President in advance.

" The latter gave the Senator and myself a
15   (225)

cordial but brief salutation, and turning immediately to the lad, said, 'And who 'is the little
boy ?'

"During their conference the Senator and myself were apparently forgotten. The boy soon
told his story, which was in substance that he had
come to Washington seeking employment as a
page in the House of Representatives, and he
wished the President to give him such an ap
pointment. To this the President replied that
such appointments were not at his disposal, and
that application must be made to the door-keeper
of the House at the Capitol.

"'But, sir,' said the lad, still undaunted, 'I am
a good boy, and have a letter from my mother,
and one from the supervisors of my town, and
one from my Sunday-school teacher; they all
told me that I could earn enough in one session of
Congress to keep my mother and the rest of us
comfortable all the remainder of the year.'

"The President took the lad's papers and ran
his eye over them with that penetrating and ab-
sorbent look so familiar to all who knew him, and
then took his pen and wrote upon the back of one
of them. 'If Capt. Goodnow can give a place to

this good little boy, I shall be gratified,' and signed it 'A. Lincoln.'

" The boy's face became radiant with hope, and he walked out of the room with a step as light as though all the angels were whispering their congratulations.

" Only after the lad had gone did the President seem to realize that a Senator and another person had been for some time waiting to see him.

" 'Think for a moment of the President of a great nation, and that nation engaged in one of the most terrible wars waged against men, himself worn down with anxiety and labor, subjected to the alternations of success and defeat, racked by complaints of the envious, the disloyal, and the unreasonable, pressed to the decision of grave questions of public policy, and encumbered by the numberless and nameless incidents of civil and martial responsibility, yet able so far to forget them all as to give himself up for the time being to the errand of a little boy, who had braved an interview uninvited, and of whom he knew nothing, but that he had a story to tell of his mother and of his ambition to serve her."

Of a different character, but equally character-

istic of Mr. Lincoln, is a story told by General
Charles G. Dahlgren, brother of Admiral Dahlgren :

"As Mr. Lincoln and my brother were about
to go to dinner, and while the President was
washing his hands, Secretary Stanton entered ex-
citedly with a telegram in his hand and said, 'Mr.
President, I have just received a dispatch from
Portland that Jake Thompson is there waiting to
take the steamer to England and I want to arrest
him.' Mr. Lincoln began to wipe his hands on a
towel, and said, in a long, drawling voice, 'Better let him slide.'

"'But, Mr. President,' said Secretary Stanton,
'this man is one of the chief traitors—was one of
Buchanan's Cabinet, betrayed the country then,
and has fought against us ever since. He should
be punished.'

"'W-e-l-l,' said the President, 'if Jake Thompson is satisfied with the issue of the war, I am.
B-e-t-t-e-r let him slide.'

"'Such men should be punished to the full extent of the law,' said Mr. Stanton. 'Why, if we
don't punish the leaders of the rebellion, what
shall we say to their followers ?'

"B-e-t-t-e-r let them slide, Stanton,' said the President, laying aside his towel.

"Mr. Stanton went out, evidently annoyed, and Mr. Lincoln, turning to my brother, said: 'Dahl, that is one of the things I don't intend to allow. When the war is over, I want it to stop, and let both sides go to work and heal the wounds, which, Heaven knows, are bad enough; but jogging and pulling them is not the best way to heal a sore.'

"And the old General, turning to his work, said, with a sigh, 'If that policy had been carried out, the wounds would have healed long ago.'"

The following story, told by M. J. Ramsdell, shows that Mr. Lincoln judged men sometimes by their spirit rather than their military qualifications:

"A sergeant of infantry, whom I shall call Dick Gower, commanded his company in a great many battles in the West in the early days of the war. His company officers had all been killed, but right royally did Dick handle his men. At the first lull in the campaign, the officers of his regiment, of his brigade, and of his division, united in recommending him for a lieutenancy in the regular army. The commanding officer joined in the recommendation. Mr. Lincoln ordered the appointment. Forthwith, Sergeant Dick was ordered before an examining board here in Washington, for the regular army officers were tenacious of what they thought their superiority. Dick presented himself in a soiled and faded sergeant's uniform, his face and hands bronzed and cracked by the winds and suns of a hot campaign.

"The curled darling of Washington society, the perfumed graduates of West Point, who had never seen a squadron set in the field, conducted the examination to ascertain if Dick was fit to be an officer in the regular army. They asked him questions as to engineering, mathematics, philosophy, and ordnance, of harbor warfare, of field campaigns, and all such stuff. Not a single question could Dick answer. 'What is an echelon?' was asked. 'I don't know,' answered Dick; 'I never saw one.' 'What is an abbattis?' was the next question? Dick answered: 'You've got me again. We haven't got 'em in the West.' 'Well, what is a hollow square?' continued his tormentors. 'Don't know,' said Dick sorrowfully; 'I never heard of one.' 'Well,' finally said a young snip in eye-glasses, 'what would you do in command of a company if the cavalry should charge on you?' They had at last got down to Dick's comprehension, and he answered with a resolute face and a flashing eye, 'I'd give them Jesse, that's what I'd do, and I'd make a hollow square in every mother's son of them.' A few more technical questions were asked, but poor Dick was not able to answer them, and the examination closed.

"The report was duly sent to the Secretary of War, who submitted it to Mr. Lincoln, saying that evidently Dick would not do for an officer. Mr. Lincoln, when through with the report, and found that Dick had not answered a single question, but he came to where Dick said what he would do if attacked by cavalry, and then he did what sensible Abe Lincoln did in all such matters, he threw the report on his table and made a little memorandum in pencil ordering the Secretary of War to appoint Dick Gower a lieutenant in the regular army. Dick achieved distinction afterward, and was everywhere known in the army as a man without fear, who never made a mistake."

A correspondent of the Boston *Traveller* fur-
nishes a humorous story told by President Lin
coln, to show the embarrassment which he felt as
to the disposal of Jefferson Davis :

" A gentleman told me a story recently whicl
well illustrates Lincoln's immense fund of anecdotes.   Said he : 'Just after Jeff Davis had been
captured I called over at the White House to see
President Lincoln.   I was ushered in, and asked
him : " Well, Mr. President, what are you going
to do with Jeff Davis ?"   Lincoln looked at me
for a moment, and then said, in his peculiar, humorous way : " That reminds me of a story.   A
boy 'way out West caught a coon and tamed it to
a considerable extent, but the animal created such
mischief about the house that his mother ordered
him to take it away and not to come home until
he could return without his pet.   The boy went
down-town with the coon, secured with a strong
piece of twine, and in about an hour he was found
sitting on the edge of the curbstone, holding the
coon with one hand and crying as though his
heart would break.   A big-hearted gentleman,
who was passing, stopped and kindly inquired :
'Say, little boy, what is the matter ?'   The boy

wiped a tear from his eye with his sleeve, and in an injured tone, howled: 'Matter! Ask me what's the matter! You see that coon there? Well, I don't know what to do with the darn thing. I can't sell it, I can't kill it, and ma won't let me take it home.' That," continued Lincoln, "is precisely my case. I am like the boy with the coon. I can't sell him, I can't kill him, and I can't take him home!" ' "

I have already remarked that Mr. Lincoln was superstitious. He seemed to be deeply impressed by dreams, and claimed to be notified in this way of the approach of important events.

"On the Friday of his death he called his Cabinet together at noon, and he seemed dispirited. He said: 'I wish I could hear from Sherman.' General Grant, who was present, said: 'You will hear well from Sherman.' He said: 'I don't know. I have had a dream, the same that I had before the battles of Bull Run, of Chancellorsville, and of Swan River. It has,' he said, 'always boded disaster.' It made a great impression on all of the Cabinet and on General Grant. Mr. Lincoln had been remonstrated with for going about unattended, but he said: 'What is the use of precautions? If they want to kill me they will kill me.' He was killed, but history will place him next to Washington in the list of beloved Presidents. The skill displayed by him in managing Chase, Stanton, Sumner, Fessenden, Wade, Seward, and other candidates for the Presidency, was wonderful, and when there was any hitch he was reminded of a story, illustrating the situation. His stories were, in short, ' parables.' "—*Boston Budget.*

Even in the hour of victory he was thoughtful, not jubilant.

"When General Weitzel escorted President Lincoln and his companions through the Capitol at Richmond the day after the occupation, in April, 1865, they reached what the rebels called the Cabinet room of the great President of the Southern Confederacy. General Weitzel said: 'This, Mr. President, is the chair which has been so long occupied by President Davis.' He pulled it from the table and motioned the President to sit down. Mr. Lincoln's face took an extra look of care and melancholy. The narrator says ' he looked at it a moment and slowly approached and wearily sat down. It was an hour of exultation with the soldiers ; we felt that the war was ended, and we knew that all over the North bells were pealing, cannon booming, and the people were delirious with joy over the prospect of peace. I expected to see the President manifest some spirit of triumph as he sat in the seat so long occupied by the rebel Government ; but his great head fell into his broad hand and a sigh that seemed to come from the soul of a nation, escaped his lips and saddened every man present. His mind seemed to be travelling back through the dark years of the war, and he was counting the cost in treasure, life, and blood that made it possible for him to sit there. As he rose without a word and left the room slowly and sadly, tears involuntarily came to the eyes of every man present, and we soldiers realized that we had not done all the suffering nor made all the sacrifices.' "

Where Abraham Lincoln obtained some of his anti-slavery ideas may be learned from a recent article in the *Century*, by Leonard W. Bacon, who describes the effects of his father's writings upon this subject on the mind of the future President :

" ' These essays '—from the preface to which I have just quoted—had been written at divers

times from 1833 onward, and were collected, in
1846, into a volume which has had a history. It
is a book of exact definitions, just discriminations,
lucid and tenacious arguments; and it deals with
certain obstinate and elusive sophistries in an ef-
fective way. It is not to be wondered at that when
it fell into the hands of a young Western lawyer,
Abraham Lincoln,—whose characteristic was 'not
to be content with an idea until he could bound
it north, east, south, and west,'—it should prove
to be a book exactly after his mind. It was to
him not only a study on slavery, but a model in
the rhetoric of debate. It is not difficult to trace
the influence of it in that great stump-debate with
Douglas, in which Lincoln's main strength lay in
his cautious wisdom in declining to take the extreme positions into which his wily antagonist
tried to provoke or entice him. When, many
years after the little book had been forgotten by
the public, and after slavery had fallen before the
President's proclamation, it appeared from Lincoln's own declaration to Dr. Joseph P. Thompson that he owed to that book his definite, reasonable, and irrefragable views on the slavery question, my father felt to sing the *Nunc dimittis.*"

CHAPTER XXVI.

MARTIAL law is severe, and, doubtless, not without reason. Desertion in time of war is a capital offence, and many a poor fellow suffered the penalty during the terrible four years of the civil war. Many more would have suffered but for the humane interposition of the President, who was glad to find the slightest excuse for saving the life of the unfortunate offender. As Dr. Holland observes, he had the deepest sympathy for the soldiers who were fighting the battles of their country. He knew something of their trials and privations, their longing for home, and the strength of the temptation which sometimes led them to lapse from duty. There was infinite tenderness in the heart of this man which made him hard to consent to extreme punishment.

(237)

I propose to cull from different sources illustrations of Mr. Lincoln's humanity. The first I find in a letter written to Dr. Holland by a personal friend of the President:

"I called on him one day in the early part of the war. He had just written a pardon for a young man who had been sentenced to be shot, for sleeping at his post as a sentinel. He remarked as he read it to me, 'I could not think of going into eternity with the blood of the poor young man on my skirts.' Then he added, 'It is not to be wondered at that a boy, raised on a farm, probably in the habit of going to bed at dark, should, when required to watch, fall asleep, and I can not consent to shoot him for such an act.'"

Dr. Holland adds that Rev. Newman Hall, of London, in a sermon preached upon and after Mr. Lincoln's death, says that the dead body of this youth was found among the slain on the field of Fredericksburg, wearing next his heart the photograph of his preserver, beneath which he had written, "God bless President Lincoln." On another occasion, when Mr. Lincoln was asked to assent to the capital punishment of twenty-four deserters, sentenced to be shot for desertion, he said to the General who pleaded the necessity of enforcing discipline, "No, General, there are already too many weeping widows in the United States. For God's sake, don't ask me to add to the number, for I won't do it."

From Mr. Carpenter's "Six Months at the White House," I make the following extract:

"The Secretary of War and Generals in command were frequently much annoyed at being overruled,—the discipline and efficiency of the service being thereby, as they considered, greatly endangered. But there was no going back of the simple signature, 'A. Lincoln,' attached to proclamation or reprieve.

"My friend Kellogg, Representative from Essex County, New York, received a dispatch one evening from the army, to the effect that a young townsman who had been induced to enlist through his instrumentality, had, for a serious misdemeanor, been convicted by a court-martial, and was to be shot the next day. Greatly agitated, Mr. Kellogg went to the Secretary of War, and urged in the strongest manner, a reprieve.

"Stanton was inexorable.

"'Too many cases of the kind had been let

off,' he said; 'and it was time an example was made.'

" Exhausting his eloquence in vain, Mr. Kellogg said: 'Well, Mr. Secretary, the boy is not going to be *shot*—of that I give you fair warning!'

"Leaving the War Department, he went directly to the White House, although the hour was late. The sentinel on duty told him that special orders had been issued to admit no one that night. After a long parley, by pledging himself to assume the responsibility of the act, the Congressman passed in. The President had retired; but, indifferent to etiquette or ceremony, Judge Kellogg pressed his way through all obstacles to his sleeping apartment. In an excited manner he stated that the dispatch announcing the hour of execution had but just reached him.

"'This man must not be shot, Mr. President,' said he. 'I can't help what he may have done. Why, he is an old neighbor of mine; I can't allow him to be shot!'

"Mr. Lincoln had remained in bed, quietly listening to the vehement protestations of his old friend (they were in Congress together). He at length said, 'Well, I don't believe *shooting* him will do him any good. Give me that **pen**. And, so saying, ' red tape ' was unceremoniously cut, and another poor fellow's lease of life was indefinitely extended.''

I continue to quote from Mr. Carpenter:

" One night Speaker Colfax left all other busi- ness to ask the President to respite the son of a constituent who was sentenced to be shot at Dav- enport for desertion. He heard the story with his usual patience, though he was wearied out with incessant calls and anxious for rest, and then replied, ' Some of our generals complain that I impair discipline and subordination in the army by my pardons and respites, but it makes me rested after a hard day's work if I can find some good excuse for saving a man's life, and I go to bed happy, as I think how joyous the signing of my name will make him and his family and his friends.'

" The Hon. Thaddeus Stevens told me that on one occasion he called at the White House with an elderly lady in great trouble, whose son had been in the army, but for some offence had been court-martialed, and sentenced either to death or imprisonment at hard labor for a long term.

There were some extenuating circumstances:
and, after a full hearing, the President turned to
the Representative, and said:

"'Mr. Stevens, do you think this is a case
which will warrant my interference?'

"'With my knowledge of the facts and the
parties,' was the reply, 'I should have no hesitation in granting a pardon.'

"'Then,' returned Mr. Lincoln, 'I will pardon
him,' and he proceeded forthwith to execute the
paper.

"The gratitude of the mother was too deep for
expression, and not a word was said between her
and Mr. Stevens until they were half-way down-
stairs on their passage out, when she suddenly
broke forth in an excited manner with the words,
'I knew it was a copperhead lie!'

"'What do you refer to, madam?' asked Mr.
Stevens.

"'Why, they told me he was an ugly-looking
man!' she replied with vehemence. 'He is the
handsomest man I ever saw in my life!'

"Doubtless the grateful mother voiced the
feeling of many another, who, in the rugged and
care-worn face had read the sympathy and goodness of the inner nature."

Another Case

"A young man connected with a New York regiment had become to all appearances a hardened criminal. He had deserted two or three times, and, when at last detected and imprisoned, had attempted to poison his guards, one of whom subsequently died from the effects of the poison unconsciously taken. Of course, there seemed no defence possible in such a case. But the fact came out that the boy had been of unsound mind.

"Some friends of his mother took up the matter, and an appeal was made to the Secretary of War. He declined positively to listen to it,— the case was too aggravating. The prisoner (scarcely more than a boy) was confined at Elmira, N. Y. The day for the execution of his sentence had nearly arrived, when his mother made her way to the President. He listened to her story, examined the record, and said that his opinion accorded with that of the Secretary of War; he could do nothing for her.

"Heart-broken, she was compelled to relinquish her last hope. One of the friends who had become interested, upon learning the result of the application, waited upon Senator Harris. That gentleman said that his engagements utterly precluded his going to see the President upon the subject, until twelve o'clock of the second night following. This brought the time to Wednesday night, and the sentence was to be executed on Thursday. Judge Harris, true to his word, called at the White House at twelve o'clock on Wednesday night. The President had retired, but the interview was granted. The point made was that the boy was insane,—thus irresponsible, and his execution would be murder. Pardon was not asked, but a reprieve, until a proper medical examination could be made.

" This was so reasonable that Mr. Lincoln acquiesced in its justice. He immediately ordered a telegram sent to Elmira, delaying the execution of the sentence. Early the next morning he sent another by a different line, and, before the hour of execution had arrived, he had sent no less than four different reprieves by different lines to different individuals in Elmira, so fearful was he that the message would fail or be too late."

These are but a few of the stories that have been told in illustration of President Lincoln's humanity. Whatever may have been the opinion of the generals in command, as to the expediency of his numerous pardons, they throw a beautiful light upon his character, and will endear his memory to all who can appreciate his tender sympathy for all, and his genuine and unaffected goodness.

CHAPTER XXVII.

ANECDOTES OF MR. LINCOLN.

A MAN's character often is best disclosed by trifling incidents, and it is for this reason, perhaps, that the public is eager to read anecdotes of its illustrious men. I shall devote the present chapter to anecdotes of President Lincoln, gathered from various quarters. I shall not use quotation-marks, but content myself with saying at the outset that they are all borrowed.

At the reception at the President's house one afternoon, many persons present noticed three little girls poorly dressed, the children of some mechanic or laboring man, who had followed the visitors fully into the house to gratify their curiosity. They passed round from room to room, and were hastening through the reception-room with some trepidation when the President called to them, " Little girls, are you going to pass me without shaking hands?"

Then he bent his tall, awkward form down, and shook each little girl warmly by the hand. Everybody in the apartment was spell-bound by the incident—so simple in itself, yet revealing so much of Mr. Lincoln's character.

The President and the Paymaster.

One of the numerous paymasters at Washington sought an introduction to Mr. Lincoln. He arrived at the White House quite opportunely, and was introduced to the President by the United States Marshal, with his blandest smile. While shaking hands with the President the paymaster remarked :

"I have no official business with you, Mr. President; I only called to pay my compliments."

" I understand," was the reply, " and, from the complaints of the soldiers, I think that is all you do pay."

The Interviewer.

An interviewer, with the best intentions in the world, once went to Mr. Lincoln's room in the

White House while he was President, and inquired:

"Mr. President, what do you think of the war
and its end?"

To which Mr. Lincoln politely and laughingly
replied:

"That question of yours puts me in mind of a
story about something which happened down in
Egypt, in the southern part of Illinois."

The point of it was that a man burned his fin-
gers by being in too much haste. Mr. Lincoln
told the story admirably well, walking up and
down the room, and heartily laughing all the
while. The interviewer was quick to see the
point. As a matter of course he was cut to the
quick, and quickly down-stairs he rushed, saying
to himself:

"I'll never interview that man again."

How Mr. Lincoln secured a Ride.

When Abraham Lincoln was a poor lawyer, he
found himself one cold day at a village some distance from Springfield, and with no means of
conveyance.

Seeing a gentleman driving along the Springfield road in a carriage, he ran up to him and politely said :

" Sir, will you have the goodness to take my overcoat to town for me ? "

" With pleasure," answered the gentleman. " But how will you get it again ? "

" Oh, very easily," said Mr. Lincoln, " as I intend to remain in it."

" Jump in," said the gentleman laughing. And the future President had a pleasant ride.

The President's Influence.

Judge Baldwin, of California, an old and highly respectable and sedate gentleman, called on General Halleck, and, presuming on a familiar acquaintance in California a few years since, solicited a pass outside of the lines to see a brother in Virginia, not thinking he would meet with a refusal, as both his brother and himself were good Union men.

" We have been deceived too often," said General Halleck, " and I regret I can't grant it."

Judge B. then went to Stanton, and was very briefly disposed of with the same result.

Finally he obtained an interview with Mr. Lincoln and stated his case.

" Have you applied to General Halleck ? " said the President.

" And met with a flat refusal," said Judge B.

" Then you must see Stanton," continued the President.

"I have, and with the same result," was the reply.

" Well, then," said the President, with a smile of good humor, "I can do nothing, for you must know that I have very little influence with this administration."

The German Lieutenant.

A lieutenant, whom debts compelled to leave his father-land, succeeded in being admitted to President Lincoln, and, by reason of his commendable and winning deportment and intelligent appearance, was promised a lieutenant's commission in a cavalry regiment.

He was so enraptured with his success, that he deemed it a duty to inform the President that he belonged to one of the oldest noble houses in Germany.

"Oh, never mind that," said Mr. Lincoln, with a twinkle of the eye; "you will not find that to be any obstacle to your advancement."

A Pass for Richmond.

A gentleman called on the President, and solicited a pass for Richmond.

"Well," said Mr. Lincoln, "I would be very happy to oblige you if my passes were respected; but the fact is, sir, I have, within the last two years, given passes to two hundred and fifty thousand men to go to Richmond, and not one has got there yet."

Mr. Lincoln and the Preacher.

An officer under the Government called at the Executive Mansion, accompanied by a clerical friend.

"Mr. President," said he, "allow me to present to you my friend, the Rev. Mr. F., of ———. Mr. F. has expressed a desire to see you, and have some conversation with you, and I am happy to be the means of introducing him."

The President shook hands with Mr. F., desired him to be seated, and took a seat himself. Then

—his countenance having assumed an expression of patient waiting—he said: "I am now ready to hear what you have to say."

"Oh, bless you, sir," said Mr. F., "I have nothing special to say. I merely called to pay my respects to you, and, as one of the million, to assure you of my hearty sympathy and support."

"My dear sir," said the President, rising promptly, his face showing instant relief, and with both hands grasping that of his visitor, "I am very glad to see you; I am *very* glad to see you, indeed. I thought you had come to preach to me."

Mr. Lincoln and his Advisers.

Some gentlemen from the West waited upon the President. They were in a critical mood. They felt that things were not going on as they should, and they wanted to give advice. The President heard them patiently, and then replied:

"Gentlemen, suppose all the property you were worth was in gold, and you had put it in the hands of Blondin to carry across the Niagara River on a rope; would you shake the cable, or keep shouting out to him—'Blondin, stand up a

little straighter!' 'Blondin, stoop a little more!'
'Go a little faster!' 'Lean a little more to the
North!' 'Lean a little more to the South!' No,
you would hold your breath as well as your tongue,
and keep your hands off till he was safely over.
The Government is carrying an immense weight.
Untold treasures are in its hands. It is doing the
best it can. Don't badger it. Keep silence, and
we'll get you safe across."

This simple illustration answered the complaints
of half an hour, and not only silenced but charmed
the audience.

Somewhat similar is the answer made to a
Western farmer, who waited upon Mr. Lincoln,
with a plan for the successful prosecution of the
war, to which the Rresident listened with as much
patience as he could. When he was through, he
asked the opinion of the President upon his plan.

" Well," said Mr. Lincoln, " I'll answer by telling you a story. You have heard of Mr. Blank,
of Chicago? He was an immense loafer in his
way—in fact, never did anything in his life. One
day he got crazy over a great rise in the price of
wheat, upon which many wheat-speculators gained
large fortunes. Blank started off one morning to

one of the most successful of the wheat speculators, and, with much enthusiasm, laid before him a plan by which he (the said Blank) was certain of becoming independently rich. When he had finished he asked the opinion of his hearer upon his plan of operations. The reply came as follows: 'I advise you to stick to your business.' 'But,' asked Blank, 'what is my business?' 'I don't know, I'm sure, what it is,' said the merchant, 'but whatever it is, I advise you to stick to it.'

"And now," said Mr. Lincoln, "I mean nothing offensive, for I know you mean well, but I think you had better stick to your business, and leave the war to those who have the responsibility of managing it."

It is said that Mr. Gladstone, the English premier, is known for his skill in chopping wood. The following anecdote shows that President Lincoln also was not without experience in the same direction:

During one of the last visits that he made to James River, a short time before the capture of Richmond, he spent some time in walking around among the hospitals, and in visiting various fatigue parties at work in putting up cabins and other buildings.

He came upon one squad who were cutting logs for a house; and chatting a moment with the hardy woodsmen, asked one of them to let him take his axe. Mr. Lincoln grasped the helve with the easy air of one perfectly familiar with the tool, and remarked that he used to be "good on the chop."

The President then let in on a big log, making the chips fly, and making as smooth a cut as the best lumberman in Maine could do.

Meantime, the men crowded round to see the work; and, as he handed back the axe, and walked away with a pleasant joke, the choppers gave him three as hearty cheers as he ever heard in the whole of his political career.

CHAPTER XXVIII.

PRESIDENT LINCOLN AS A RELIGIOUS MAN.

Soon after the death of Mr. Lincoln, Mr. Noah Brooks published in *Harper's Monthly* an interesting article, devoted to reminiscences of his dead friend. From this article, I make a few extracts, for which my readers will thank me:

"Just after the last Presidential election, he said: 'Being only mortal, after all, I should have been a little mortified if I had been beaten in this canvass; but that sting would have been more than compensated by the thought that the people had notified me that all my official responsibilities were soon to be lifted off my back.' In reply to the remark that in all these cares he was daily remembered by all who prayed, not to be heard of men, as no man had ever before been remembered, he caught at the homely phrase, and said, ' Yes, I like that phrase, " not to be heard of men," and, again, it is generally true as you say; at least I have been told so, and I have been a good deal helped by just that thought.' Then he solemnly and slowly added: 'I should be the most presumptuous blockhead upon this footstool, if I, for one day, thought that I could discharge the duties which have come upon me since I came into this place, without the aid and enlightenment of One who is stronger and wiser than all others.' "

" At another time he said cheerfully, ' I am very sure that if I do not go away from here a wise man, I shall go away a better man, for having learned here what a very poor sort of man I am.' Afterward, referring to what he called a change of heart, he said he did not remember any precise time when he passed through any special change of purpose or heart; but he would say, that his own election to office, and the crisis immediately following, influentially determined him in what he called 'a process of crystallization' then going on in his mind. Reticent as he was, and shy of discoursing much of his own mental exercises, these few utterances now have a value with those who knew him, which his dying words would scarcely have possessed."

"On Thursday of a certain week, two ladies from Tennessee came before the President, asking the release of their husbands, held as prisoners of war at Johnson's Island. They were put off until Friday, when they came again, and were again put off until Saturday. At each of the interviews one of the ladies urged that her husband was a religious man. On Saturday, when the President ordered the release of the prisoner, he said to this lady : ' You say your husband is a religious man : tell him, when you meet him, that I say I am not much of a judge of religion, but that, in my opinion, the religion which sets men to rebel and fight against their Government, because, as they think, that Government does not sufficiently help *some* men to eat their bread in the sweat of other men's faces, is not the sort of religion upon which people can get to heaven.' "

" On an occasion I shall never forget," says the Hon. H. C. Denning, of Connecticut, " the conversation turned upon religious subjects, and Mr. Lincoln made this impressive remark : ' I have never united myself to any church, because I have found difficulty in giving my assent, without men-

tal reservation, to the long, complicated statements of Christian doctrine which characterize
their Articles of Belief and Confessions of Faith.
When any church will inscribe over its altar, as
its sole qualification of membership, the Saviour's
condensed statement of the substance of both
Law and Gospel, "Thou shalt love the Lord thy
God with all thy heart, and with all thy soul, and
thy neighbor as thyself," that church will I join
with all my heart and with all my soul.'"

Though Mr. Lincoln never formally united
himself with any church, doubtless for the reason given above, because he knew of none broad
and tolerant enough for him, it is clear that his
mind was much occupied with matters connected
with religion. No one could charge him with
scoffing at sacred things. Had he even been so
inclined, the bereavement which visited him in
the death of his son Willie, who died February
20th, 1862, would assuredly have changed him.
Devoted as he was to his children, this loss affected him deeply, and it was not till several
weeks had passed that he was in any measure rec-
onciled.

"Gentlemen," said one of the guests at a dinner-party in Washington, during which the President had been freely discussed, " you may talk as you please about Mr. Lincoln's capacity. I don't believe him to be the ablest statesman in America, by any means, and I voted against him on both occasions of his candidacy. But I happened to see, or rather to hear, something the other day that convinced me that, however deficient he may be in the head, he is all right in the heart. I was up at the White House, having called to see the President on business. I was shown into the office of his private secretary, and told that Mr. Lincoln was busy just then, but would be disengaged in a short time. While waiting, I heard a very earnest prayer being uttered in a loud female voice in the adjoining room. I inquired what it meant, and was told that an old Quaker lady, a friend of the President's, had called that afternoon and taken tea at the White House, and that she was then praying with Mr. Lincoln. After the lapse of a few minutes the prayer ceased, and the President, accompanied by a Quakeress, not less than eighty years old, entered the room where I was sitting. I made up my mind then, gentlemen, that Mr. Lincoln was not a bad man; and I don't think it will be easy to efface the impression that the scene I witnessed, and the voice I heard, made upon my mind!"

To some members of the Christian Commission who were calling upon him, Mr. Lincoln said: "If it were not for my firm belief in an over-ruling Providence, it would be difficult for me, in the midst of such complications of affairs, to keep my reason on its seat. But I am confident that the Almighty has His plans, and will work them out; and, whether we see it or not, they will be the wisest and best for us. I have always taken counsel of Him, and referred to Him my plans, and have never adopted a course of pro-ceeding without being assured, as far as I could be, of His approbation. To be sure, He has not conformed to my desires, or else we should have been out of our trouble long ago. On the other hand, His will does not seem to agree with the wish of our enemy over there (pointing across the Poto-mac). He stands the Judge between us, and we ought to be willing to accept His decision. We have reason to anticipate that it will be favorable to us, for our cause is right."

It was during this interview, as Dr. Holland

tells us, that the fact was privately communicated to a member of the Commission that Mr. Lincoln was in the habit of spending an early hour each day in prayer.

It will hardly be necessary, after the reader has read thus far, to answer the charge made in some quarters that Mr. Lincoln was an infidel. Few of his critics possess his simple faith in God and his deep reverence for the Almighty, whose instrument he firmly believed himself to be. I can not deny myself the satisfaction of reproducing here Dr. Holland's remarks upon the life and character of the President:

"Mr. Lincoln's character was one which will grow. It will become the basis of an ideal man. It was so pure, and so unselfish, and so rich in its materials, that fine imaginations will spring from it to blossom and bear fruit through all the centuries. This element was found in Washington, whose human weaknesses seem to have faded entirely from memory, leaving him a demi-god; and it will be found in Mr. Lincoln to a still more remarkable degree. The black race have already crowned him. With the black man, and particularly the black freedman, Mr. Lincoln's name is the

saintliest which he pronounces, and the noblest
he can conceive. To the emancipated he is more
than man—a being scarcely second to the Lord
Jesus Christ himself. That old, white-headed
negro, who undertook to tell what 'Massa Linkum' was to his dark-minded brethren, embodied
the vague conceptions of his race in the words:
'Massa Linkum, he ebery whar; he know ebery
ting; he walk de earf like de Lord.' He was to
these men the incarnation of power and goodness;
and his memory will live in the hearts of this unfortunate and oppressed race while it shall exist
upon the earth."

While the names of Lincoln and Washington
are often associated, the former holds a warmer
place in the affections of the American people
than his great predecessor, who, with all his ex-
cellence, was far removed by a certain coldness
and reserve from the sympathies of the common
people. Abraham Lincoln, on the other hand,
was always accessible, and his heart overflowed
with sympathy for the oppressed and the lowly.
The people loved him, for they felt that he was
one of themselves.

CHAPTER XXIX.

EMANCIPATING THE SLAVES.

THE "great central act" of Mr. Lincoln's administration, as he himself calls it, was the emancipation of the slaves. At the stroke of a pen the shackles fell from four millions of persons in a state of servitude. On the 1st of January, 1863, emancipation was proclaimed, and the promise was made that "the Executive Government of the United States, including the military and naval authorities thereof, will recognize and maintain the freedom of said persons."

This important proclamation carried joy, not only to the persons most interested, but to the friends of Freedom everywhere.

Mr. Lincoln had been importuned to take this step before. Earnest anti-slavery men like Charles Sumner and Horace Greeley felt that he delayed

too long; but the President was wiser than they.
He had always been an anti-slavery man, but his
own wishes did not give him the right to abolish slavery. I can not do better than to give
Mr. Lincoln's reasons for the course he pursued,
in his own words, spoken to George Thompson,
an eminent English anti-slavery man, in April,
1864:

"Mr. Thompson," said the President, "the
people of Great Britain and of other foreign governments were in one great error in reference to
this conflict. They seemed to think that, the
moment I was President, I had the power to
abolish slavery, forgetting that, before I could
have any power whatever, I had to take the oath
to support the Constitution of the United States,
and execute the laws as I found them. When
the Rebellion broke out, my duty did not admit
of a question. I did not consider that I had a
right to touch the 'State' institution of slavery
until all other measures for restoring the Union
had failed. The paramount idea of the Constitution is the preservation of the Union. It may not
be specified in so many words, but that this was
the 'idea of its founders is evident; for, without

the Union, the Constitution would be worthless. It seems clear, then, that in the last extremity, if any local institution threatened the existence of the Union, the Executive could not hesitate as to his duty.   In our case, the moment came when I felt that slavery must die—that the nation must live!   I have sometimes used the illustration in this connection of a man with a diseased limb and his surgeon.   So long as there is a chance of the patient's restoration, the surgeon is solemnly bound to try to save both life and limb; but when the crisis comes, and the limb must be sacrificed as the only chance of saving the life, no honest man will hesitate.

" Many of my strongest supporters urged Emancipation before I thought it indispensable, and, I may say, before I thought the country ready for it.   It is my conviction that, had the proclamation been issued even six months earlier than it was, public sentiment would not have sustained it.   Just so as to the subsequent action in reference to enlisting blacks in the Border States. The step, taken sooner, could not, in my judgment, have been carried out.   A man watches his pear-tree day after day, impatient for the ripening of the fruit. Let him attempt to force the process, and he may spoil both fruit and tree. But let him patiently wait, and the ripe pear at length falls into his lap! We have seen this great revolution in public sentiment slowly, but *surely*, progressing, so that, when final action came, the opposition was not strong enough to defeat the purpose. I can now solemnly assert that I have a clear conscience in regard to my action on this momentous question. I have done what no man could have helped doing, standing in my place."

I find an interesting account in Mr. Carpenter's volume, of the circumstances attending Mr. Lincoln's signing the Emancipation Proclamation, quoted, I believe, from Col. Forney. It runs thus:

"The roll containing the Emancipation Proclamation was taken to Mr. Lincoln at noon on the 1st day of January, 1863, by Secretary Seward and his son Frederick.

"As it lay unrolled before him, Mr. Lincoln took a pen, dipped it in ink, moved his hand to the place for the signature, held it a moment, and then removed his hand and dropped the pen. After a little hesitation he again took up the pen and went through the same movement as before. Mr. Lincoln then turned to Mr. Seward, and said:

" 'I have been shaking hands since nine o'clock this morning, and my right arm is almost paralyzed. If my name ever goes into history it will be for this act, and my whole soul is in it. If my hand trembles when I sign this Proclamation, all who examine the document hereafter will say, " He hesitated." '

" He then turned to the table, took up the pen again, and slowly, firmly wrote that 'Abraham Lincoln,' with which the world is now familiar. He looked up, smiled, and said: 'That will do.' "

That act linked the name of Abraham Lincoln with one of the greatest acts in all history. That act gave him an earthly immortality!

CHAPTER XXX.

In hard and incessant labor, under a burden of care and anxiety that were making him an old man before his time, the term for which Mr. Lincoln was elected President passed slowly away. And the question came to the Nation, "Who shall be our next President? Shall it be the man who has led us thus far through the wilderness, or shall we make choice of another leader?"

There was a difference of opinion. Some were in favor of Géneral Fremont, many favored Mr. Chase, the Secretary of the Treasury, and there is no doubt that both of these two eminent men wished for the office. Mr. Lincoln, too, wished to be re-elected, not, I am sure, because power was sweet, but because he wished to carry out to the end the mighty work which it had been given to him to do. He knew that Mr. Chase desired

(269)

to succeed him, but it did not make him less
friendly; nor when it devolved upon him to
appoint a successor to Chief-Justice Taney, did it
prevent him from conferring upon his chief rival
that high office.   He considered Mr. Chase, of all
men, most fit to fill the position, and that with
him was the paramount consideration.

However politicians may have differed with
regard to the Presidency, the people were with
Mr. Lincoln.   They had learned to trust him, and
the politicians were obliged to acquiesce in their
choice.   He was nominated, and duly elected, and
the country breathed more freely.   It was an as-
surance that the war would proceed till the rebellion was crushed out, and the restoration of the
Union was now looked upon, under God, as certain.

During the campaign, Senator Sherman, of
Ohio, in a speech at Sandusky, gave this rough
but accurate sketch of Mr. Lincoln and his claims
to support.   It was addressed to a Western
audience, and doubtless produced a powerful impression:

"I know old Abe," said the Senator, "and I
tell you there is not, at this hour, a more patriotic

or a truer man living than that man Abraham
Lincoln. Some say he is an imbecile; but he not
only held his own in his debates with Douglas,
whose power is admitted, and whom I considered
the ablest intellect in the United States Senate,
but got a little the better of him. He has been
deliberate and slow, but when he puts his foot
down it is with the determination and certainty
with which our generals take their steps; and,
like them, when he takes a city he never gives it
up. This firm old man is noble and kind-hearted.
He is a child of the people. Go to him with a
story of woe, and he will weep like a child. This
man so condemned works more hours than any
President that ever occupied the chair. His
solicitude for the public welfare is never-ceasing.
I differed from him at first myself, but at last
felt and believed that he was right, and shall vote
for this brave, true, patriotic, kind-hearted man.
All his faults and mistakes you have seen; all his
virtues you never can know. His patience in
labor is wonderful. He works far harder than any
man in Erie County. At the head of this great
nation—look at it! He has all the bills to sign
passed by Congress. No one can be appointed to

any office without his approval. No one can be punished without the judgment receives his sig-nature, and no one pardoned without his hand. This man—always right, always just—we propose to re-elect now to the Presidency."

CHAPTER XXXI.

THE SPEECH AT GETTYSBURG.

ONE of the most important and critical battles of the Civil War took place on the soil of Pennsylvania. The battle of Gettysburg commenced on the 1st day of July, 1863, and lasted for three days. The invasion of Pennsylvania by Lee's forces was a bold turning of the tables upon the Federal forces, but fortunately they had a brave, cool, and skillful commander in General Meade, who beat back the Confederates with terrible loss.

It is needless to say that excitement, amounting to panic, prevailed throughout the North. Had Lee been successful in his bold movement, he would probably have continued his victories through the State, and menaced more than one Northern city. The danger was averted, but the victory was won at large cost. The Federal loss in dead, wounded, and missing amounted to twenty-three thousand, though considerably less than the losses on the other side. A piece of land adjoining the cemetery of the town was given by the State as a last resting-place for the loyal soldiers who had fallen in the battle, and on the 19th of November it was dedicated. Two addresses were made—one by Hon. Edward Everett, which was not unworthy of the eminent Massachusetts orator; but the second, though brief, was a gem which will live longer than the stately periods of Everett. It was by President Lincoln himself, and surprised even those who best appreciated him. There are few of my readers to whom it is not familiar, but I can not deny myself the pleasure of recording it here:

"Four score and seven years ago," said Mr. Lincoln, "our fathers brought forth upon this continent a new nation, conceived in liberty, and dedicated to the proposition that all men are created equal. Now we are engaged in a great civil war, testing whether that nation, or any nation so conceived and so dedicated, can long endure. We are met on a great battle-field of that war. We have come to dedicate a portion of that field as a final resting-place for those who here gave their lives that that nation might live. It is altogether fitting and proper that we should do this. But in a larger sense we can not dedicate, we can not consecrate, we can not hallow this ground. The brave men, living and dead, who struggled here, have consecrated it far above our power to add or detract. The world will little note, nor long remember, what we say here; but it can never forget what they did here. It is for us, the living, rather to be dedicated here to the unfinished work which they who fought here have thus far so nobly advanced. It is rather for us to be here dedicated to the great task remaining before us, that from these honored dead we take increased devotion to that cause for which they gave the last full measure of devotion; that we here highly resolve that these dead shall not have died in vain; that this nation, under God, shall have a new birth of freedom, and that the government of the people, by the people, and for the people shall not perish from the earth."

Is there anything to be found in the addresses of any orator, ancient or modern, more elevated in sentiment or admirable in expression? Yet the speaker had been reared in the backwoods, a stranger to schools and colleges, and his eloquence was neither acquired nor inherited. This speech alone proclaims Abraham Lincoln a man of genius.

CHAPTER XXXII.

THE CURTAIN FALLS.

An Oriental monarch, fearing that in the plenitude of his power he might forget the common fate, engaged a trusted attendant from time to time to remind him of his mortality.

Abraham Lincoln needed no such reminder. Before his first inauguration, and at intervals during his official life, he received frequent threatening letters, menacing him with death. These he kept in a package by themselves. Though he never permitted them to influence his action, they had their natural effect upon a mind and temperament subject to despondency, and not free from superstition. Mr. Lincoln had a strong impression that he would not live through his term of office. When, however, he was inaugurated for a second time, amid the plaudits of the nation,

and the clouds of civil war seemed lifting to re-
veal a brighter future, his spirits, too, became
buoyant, and he permitted himself to believe that
all would end well, and he would be permitted to
reconcile the disaffected States, and bring them
back into the national fold.   His heart was full of
tenderness and magnanimity toward the States in
rebellion.   His large heart was incapable of har-
boring malice, or thirsting for revenge.

But he was only to come in sight of the Promised Land.   It was for another leader to finish his
weary and protracted task, and reap where he had
sown.   .

On the evening of the fourteenth of April,
1865, President Lincoln and wife with two friends
occupied a box at Ford's Theatre, by invitation
of the manager, to witness a performance of Tom
Taylor's " American Cousin."   They arrived late,
and their entrance was greeted with enthusiasm,
the large audience rising to their feet and cheer-
ing.

Not long afterward, John Wilkes Booth, a
young actor, who, throughout the war, had made
no secret of his sympathy with the Confederate
cause, entered the theatre, and, not without diffi

culty, made his way through the crowded dress circle to the back of the box in which the President's party were seated.

"The President has sent for me," he said to the servant, showing his card, and thus he gained admission.

Standing in the door-way, after a hasty glance at the interior, he took a small Derringer pistol in one hand, holding at the same time a double-edged dagger in the other, he aimed deliberately at Mr. Lincoln, who sat in an arm-chair, with his back to him. There was a quick report, and the fatal bullet had entered Mr. Lincoln's brain. Major Rathbone, the only other gentleman present in the box, quickly comprehending the truth, tried to seize the assassin, but he was too quick for him. Striking at him with his dagger, he sprang to the front of the box, leaped upon the stage, crying in a theatrical tone, "Sic semper tyrannis!" and "The South is avenged!" and, favored by his knowledge of the stage, escaped at the rear before the actors and audience, stupefied by the suddenness of his act, could arrest his flight.

Too well had the assassin done his work! The

President never spoke, or recovered consciousness.   He was carried from the theatre to a house
near at hand, where, at twenty-two minutes past
seven the next morning, he expired, with his
mourning friends around him.

On the same evening another tragedy came
near being enacted in another part of the city—a
branch, no doubt, of the same wicked conspiracy.
Mr. Seward, Secretary of State, lay sick at his
house, having been thrown from his carriage and
severely injured a few days before.   A man, who
proved to be Lewis Payne Powell, gained admission by a subterfuge, and, though warned by the
servant that no one was admitted to see Mr. Seward, pushed past him into the Secretary's chamber.   At the entrance the Secretary's son, Mr.
Frederick Seward, forbade him to enter, but Powell struck him upon the forehead with the butt of
a pistol, and, rushing to the bed, stabbed the help
less Secretary three times, and would have killed
him but for his nurse, a soldier named Robinson,
who grappled with him, receiving severe blows
in the struggle.   Powell escaped from the house,
after stabbing no less than five persons.

To describe the grief, anger, and consternation

which these two tragedies produced throughout the country, would be well-nigh impossible. Then, for the first time, it became apparent how dear to the popular heart was the plain, honest, untiring man who, for more than four dark and gloomy years, had borne the national burden, and labored as best he might to restore peace and harmony to a distracted land.

The conspirators had been only too successful, but they had not accomplished all they had in view. It had been expected that General Grant would form one of the President's party; fortunately, he had excused himself, and left the city. Could he, too, have fallen a victim, dark indeed would have been the dawning of the next day, and the wide-spread feeling of horror would have been deepened.

In a recent conversation General Grant thus speaks of this sad time : " The darkest day of my life was the day I heard of Lincoln's assassination. I did not know what it meant. Here was the rebellion put down in the field, and starting up again in the gutters; we had fought it as war, now we had to fight it as assassination. Lincoln was killed on the 14th of April. I was busy sending out orders to stop recruiting, the purchase of supplies, and to muster out the army. Lincoln had promised to go to the theatre, and wanted me to go with him. While I was with the President a letter came from Mrs. Grant, saying that she must leave Washington that night. She wanted to go to Burlington to see her children. Some incident of a trifling nature had made her resolve to leave that evening. I was glad to have it so, as I did not want to go to the theatre. So I made my excuse to Lincoln, and, at the proper hour, we started for the train. As we were driving along Pennsylvania Avenue, a horseman rode past us on a gallop, and back again around our carriage, looking into it.

"Mrs. Grant said: 'There is the man who sat near us at lunch to-day with some other men, and tried to overhear our conversation. He was so rude that we left the dining-room. Here he is now, riding after us.'

"I thought it was only curiosity, but learned afterwards that the horseman was Booth. It seemed that I was to have been attacked, and Mrs. Grant's sudden resolve to leave changed the plan. A few days after I received an anonymous letter from a man, saying that he had been detailed to kill me; that he rode on my train as far as Havre de Grace, and as my car was locked he failed to get in. He thanked God that he had failed. I remembered that the conductor had locked the car, but how true the letter was I can not say. I learned of the assassination as I was passing through Philadelphia. I turned around, took a special train, and came on to Washington. It was the gloomiest day of my life."

Of the imposing funeral ceremonies, and the manifestations of deep grief throughout the nation, I need not speak. As Dr. Holland well says: "Millions felt that they had lost a brother, or a father, or a dear personal friend. It was a grief that brought the nation more into family sympathy than it had been since the days of the Revolution. Men came together in public meetings, to give expression to their grief. . . . . There were men engaged in the rebellion who turned from the deed with horror. Many of these had learned something of the magnanimity of Mr. Lincoln's character; and they felt that the time would come when the South would need his friendship."

There is no reason to believe that the Southern leaders countenanced or instigated this atrocious deed. It was the act of a half-crazed political fanatic, and the few who were in sympathy with him, and cognizant of his plans, were men of like character. Justice overtook them in the end, as might have been expected, but they had wrought irreparable misch.ef, and plunged a whole people into mourning.

CHAPTER XXXIII

MR HERNDON'S ESTIMATE OF MR. LINCOLN,

No one probably was better fitted to give a discriminating analysis of Mr. Lincoln's character than Mr. W. H. Herndon, for more than twenty years his law-partner. From an address delivered at Springfield, Ill., Dec. 12, 1865, by that gentleman, I shall, therefore, quote freely, without indorsing everything that is said, but submitting it as the opinion of a man who knew Mr. Lincoln well:

"Mr. Lincoln read *less* and thought *more* than any man in his sphere in America. No man can put his finger on any great book written in the last or present century that he read. When young he read the Bible, and when of age he read Shakespeare. This latter book was scarcely ever out of his mind. Mr. Lincoln is acknowl-

edged to have been a great man, but the question is, What made him great? I repeat that he
read less and thought more than any man of his
standing in America, if not in the world. He
possessed originality and power of thought in an
eminent degree. He was cautious, cool, concen-
trated, with continuity of reflection; was patient
and enduring. These are some of the grounds of
his wonderful success.

"Not only was nature, man, fact, and principle
suggestive to Mr. Lincoln—not only had he accurate and exact perceptions, but he was causative;
i.e., his mind ran back behind all facts, things,
and principles to their origin, history, and first
cause,—to that point where forces act at once as
effect and cause. He would stop and stand in the
street and analyze a machine. He would whittle
things to a point, and then count the numberless
inclined planes and their pitch, making the point.
Mastering and defining this, he would then cut
that point back and get a broad transverse section
of his pine stick and point and define that. Clocks,
omnibuses, and language, paddle-wheels, and
idioms, never escaped his observation and analysis. Before he could form any idea of anything

—before he would express his opinion on any subject, he must know it in origin and history, in substance and quality, in magnitude and gravity. He must know his subject inside and outside, upside and downside. He searched his own mind and nature thoroughly, as I have often heard him say. He must analyze a sensation, an idea, and words, and run them back to their origin, history, purpose, and destiny."

" All things, facts, and principles had to run through his crucible and be tested by the fires of his analytic mind; and hence, when he did speak, his utterances rang out gold-like—quick, keen, and current—upon the counters of the understanding. He reasoned logically, through analogy and comparison. All opponents dreaded him in his originality of idea, condensation, definition, and force of expression, and woe be to the man who hugged to his bosom a secret error if Mr. Lincoln got on the chase of it! I say, woe to him! Time could hide the error in no nook or corner of space in which he would not detect and expose it."

" Mr. Lincoln was a peculiar man, having a peculiar mind. He was gifted with a peculiarity—

namely, a new lookout on nature. Everything had to be newly created for him—facts newly gathered, newly arranged, and newly classed. He had no faith, as already expressed. In order to believe, he must see and feel and thrust his hand into the place. Such a mind as this must act strongly,—must have its time. His forte and power lay in his love of digging out for himself and hunting up for his own mind its own food, to be assimilated unto itself; and then, in time, he could and would form opinions and conclusions that no human power could overthrow. They were as irresistible as iron thunder, as powerful as logic embodied in mathematics."

"An additional question naturally suggests itself here, and it is this: Had Mr. Lincoln great, good common sense? Different persons of equal capacity and honesty hold different views on this question—one class answering in the affirmative and the other in the negative.

"These various opinions necessarily spring out of the question just discussed. If the true test is that a man shall quickly, wisely, and well judge the rapid rush and whirl of human transactions as accurately as though indefinite time and proper

conditions were at his disposal, then I am compelled to follow the logic of things, and say that
Mr. Lincoln had no more than ordinary common
sense. The world, men, and their actions must
be judged as they rush and pass along. They will
not wait on us—will not stay for our logic and
analysis; they must be seized as they run. We
all our life act on the moment. Mr. Lincoln
knew himself, and never trusted his dollar or his
fame on his casual opinions; he never acted hastily on great matters."

"The great predominating elements of Mr.
Lincoln's peculiar character were—first, his great
capacity and power of reason; secondly, his excellent understanding; thirdly, an exalted idea of
the sense of right and equity; and fourthly, his
intense veneration of what was true and good.
His reason ruled despotically all other faculties
and qualities of his mind. His conscience and
heart were ruled by it. His conscience was ruled
by one faculty—reason; his heart was ruled by
two faculties—reason and conscience. I know it
is generally believed that Mr. Lincoln's heart, his
love and kindness, his tenderness and benevolence
were his ruling qualities; but this opinion is er-

roneous in every particular. First, as to his reason. He dwelt in the mind; not in the conscience, and not in the heart. He lived and
breathed and acted from his reason,—the throne
of logic and the home of principle, the realm of
Deity in man. It is from this point that Mr. Lincoln must be viewed. His views were correct and
original. He was cautious not to be deceived; he
was patient and enduring. He had concentration
and great continuity of thought; he had a pro-
found analytic power; his vision was clear, and
he was emphatically the master of statement.
His pursuit of the truth was indefatigable—terrible. He reasoned from his well-chosen principles with such clearness, force, and compactness,
that the tallest intellects in the land bowed to him
with respect. He was the strongest man I ever
saw—looking at him from the stand-point of his
reason, the throne of his logic. He came from
that height with an irresistible and crushing
force. His printed speeches will prove this;
but his speeches before courts, especially before
the Supreme Courts of the State and Nation,
would demonstrate it. Unfortunately none of
them have been preserved. Here he demanded

time to think and prepare. The office of reason is to determine the truth. Truth is the power of reason—the child of reason. He loved and idolized truth for its own sake. It was reason's food.

"Conscience, the second great quality and forte of Mr. Lincoln's character, is that faculty which loves the just. Its office is justice; right and equity are its correlatives. It decides upon all acts of all people at all times. Mr. Lincoln had a deep, broad, living conscience. His great reason told him what was true, good and bad, right, wrong, just or unjust, and his conscience echoed back its decision; and it was from this point that he acted and spoke and wove his character and fame among us. His conscience ruled his heart; he was always just before he was gracious. This was his motto—his glory; and this is as it should be. It can not be truthfully said of any mortal man that he was always just. Mr. Lincoln was not always just, but his general life was. It follows that if Mr. Lincoln had great reason and great conscience, he was an honest man. His great and general life was honest, and he was justly and righ fully entitled to the appellation, 'Honest Abe!' Honesty was his great polar star.

" Mr. Lincoln had also a good understanding;
that is, the faculty that understands and compre-
hends the exact state of things, their near and re-
mote relation.   The understanding does not necessarily inquire for the reason of things.   I must
here repeat that Mr. Lincoln was an odd and original man; he lived by himself and out of himself.
He could not absorb.   He was a very sensitive
man, unobtrusive and gentlemanly, and often hid
himself in the common mass of men, in order to
prevent the discovery of his individuality.   He
had no insulting egotism and no pompous pride;
no haughtiness and no aristocracy.   He was not
indifferent, however, to approbation and public
opinion.   He was not an upstart and had no inso-
lence.   He was a meek, quiet, unobtrusive gentleman.   These qualities of his nature merged
somewhat his identities.   Read Mr. Lincoln's
speeches, letters, messages, and proclamations;
read his whole record in his actual life, and you
can not fail to perceive that he had good understanding. He understood and fully comprehended
himself; and what he did, and why he did it, better than most living men."

" There are two opinions—radically different opinions—expressed about Mr. Lincoln's will by men of equal and much capacity. One opinion is that he had *no* will, and the other is that he was *all* will—omnipotently so. These two opinions are loudly and honestly affirmed. Mr. Lincoln's mind loved the true, the right, and good—all the great truths and principles in the mind of man. He loved the true first, the right second, and the good the least. His mind struggled for truths and his soul for substances. Neither in his heart nor in his soul did he care for forms, methods, ways, —the *non*-substantial facts or things. He could not by his very structure and formation in mind and body care anything about them. He did not intensely or much care for particular individual man—dollar, property, rank, order, manners, and such like things. He had no avarice in his nature, or other like vice. . . . . What suited a little, narrow, critical mind, did not suit Mr. Lincoln's; any more than a child's clothes did his body. Generally, Mr. Lincoln did not take any interest in little local elections—town meetings. He attended no gatherings that pertained to local or other such interests, saving general political ones. He did not care (because he could not in his nature) who succeeded to the presidency of this or that Christian Association or Railroad Convention; who made the most money; who was going to Philadelphia; when and for what; and what were the costs of such a trip. He could not care who among friends got this office or that —who got to be street inspector or alley commis-'oner. No principle of goodness, of truth, or right was here. How could he be moved by such things as these? He could not understand why men struggled for such things. He made this remark to me one day—I think at Washington: 'If ever this free people—if this Government itself is ever utterly demoralized, it will come from this human wriggle and struggle for office; a way to live, without work; from which nature I am not free myself.' It puzzled him a good deal at Washington to know and to get at the root of this dread desire,—this contagious disease of national robbery in the nation's death-struggle.

"Because Mr. Lincoln could not feel any interest in such little things as I have spoken of, nor feel any particular interest in the success of those who were then struggling and wriggling, he was called indifferent—nay, ungrateful—to his friends. Especially is this the case with men who have aided Mr. Lincoln all their life. Mr. Lincoln always and everywhere wished his friends well; he loved his friends, and clung to them tenaciously, like iron to iron welded; yet he could not be actively and energetically aroused to the true sense of his friends' particularly strong feelings of anxiety for office. From this fact Mr. Lincoln has been called ungrateful. He was not an ungrateful man by any means. He may have been a cool man—a passive man in his general life; yet he was not ungrateful. Ingratitude is too positive a word—it does not convey the truth. Mr. Lincoln may not have measured his friendly duties by the applicant's hot desire; I admit this. He was not a selfish man,—if by selfishness is meant that Mr. Lincoln would do any act, even to promote himself to the Presidency, if by that act any human being was wronged. If it is said that Abraham Lincoln preferred Abraham Lincoln to any one else in the pursuit of his ambitions, and that, because of this, he was a selfish man, then I can see no objections to such an idea, for this is universal human nature.

"It must be remembered that Mr. Lincoln's mind acted logically, cautiously, and slowly. Now, having stated the above facts, the question of his will and its power is easily solved. Be it remembered that Mr. Lincoln cared nothing for simple facts, manners, modes, ways, and such like things. Be it remembered, that he *did* care for truth, for right, for principle, for all that pertains to the good. In relation to simple facts, unrelated to substance, forms, rules, methods, ways, manners, he cared nothing; and if he could be aroused, he would do anything for anybody at any time, as well foe as friend. As a politician he would courteously grant all facts and forms—all non-essential things—to his opponent. He did so because he did not care for them; they were rubbish, husks, trash. On the question of substance, he hung and clung with all his might. On questions of truth, justice, right, the good, on principle—his will was as firm as steel and as tenacious as iron. . . . . Ask Mr Lincoln to do a wrong thing, and he would scorn the request; ask him to do an unjust thing, and he would cry 'Begone! ask him to sacrifice his

convictions of the truth, and his soul would indig-
nantly exclaim, 'The world perish first!'"

. . . .

"Mr. Lincoln sometimes walked our streets
cheerily, good-humoredly, perhaps joyously—and
then it was, on meeting a friend, he cried, 'How
d'ye?' clasping one of his friend's hands in both
of his, giving a good, hearty soul-welcome. Of
a winter's morning he might be seen stalking and
stilting it toward the market-house, basket on arm,
his old gray shawl wrapped around his neck, his
little Willie or Tad running along at his heels,
asking a thousand little quick questions, which
his father heard not, not even then knowing that
little Willie or Tad was there, so abstracted was
he. When he thus met a friend, he said that
something put him in mind of a story which he
heard in Indiana or elsewhere, and tell it he would,
and there was no alternative but to listen.

"Thus, I say, stood and walked and looked this
singular man. He was odd, but when that gray
eye and face, and every feature were lit up by the
inward soul in fires of emotion, *then* it was that
all those apparently ugly features sprang into or-

gans of beauty, or sunk themselves into a sea of inspiration that sometimes flooded his face. Sometimes it appeared to me that Lincoln's soul was just fresh from the presence of its Creator."

'' This man, this long, bony, wiry, sad man, floated into our county in 1831, in a frail canoe, down the north fork of the Sangamon River, friendless, penniless, powerless, and alone—begging for work in this city,—ragged, struggling for the common necessaries of life. This man, this peculiar man, left us, in 1861, the President of the United States, backed by friends and power, by fame and all human force; and it is well to inquire *how ?*

" To sum up, let us say, here is a sensitive, diffident, unobtrusive, natural-made gentleman. His mind was strong and deep, sincere and honest, patient and enduring; having no vices and having only negative defects, with many positive virtues. His is a strong, honest, sagacious, manly, noble life. He stands in the foremost rank of men in all ages,—their equal,—one of the best types of this Christian civilization."

CHAPTER XXXIV.

MR. LINCOLN'S FAVORITE POEM.

ONE evening when Mr. Carpenter, the artist, was alone with Mr. Lincoln in his study, the President said : " There is a poem that has been a great favorite with me for years, to which my attention was first called when a young man, by a friend, and which I afterward saw and cut from a newspaper and carried in my pocket till, by frequent reading, I had it by heart. I would give a great deal to know who wrote it, but I could never ascertain."

He then repeated the poem, now familiar to the public, commencing, " Oh ! why should the spirit of mortal be proud ? "

This poem, which was written by William Knox, a young Scotchman, a contemporary of Sir Walter Scott, suits well the thoughtful, melancholy mood habitual to Mr. Lincoln. It is said

that a man may be known by his favorite poem.
Whether this can be said of men in general may
be doubted. In the case of Abraham Lincoln I
think those who knew him best would agree that
the sadness underlying the poem found an echo
in the temperament he inherited from his mother.
I am sure my readers will be glad to find the
poem recorded here, even though they may have
met with it before:

Oh ! why should the spirit of mortal be proud ?
Like a swift-fleeting meteor, a fast-flying cloud,
A flash of the lightning, a break of the wave,
He passeth from life to his rest in the grave.

The leaves of the oak and the willow shall fade,
Be scattered around and together be laid ;
And the young and the old, the low and the high,
Shall moulder to dust, and together shall lie—

The infant a mother attended and loved ;
The mother that infant's affection who proved:
The husband, that mother and infant who blest—
Each, all, are away to their dwellings of rest.

The maid on whose cheek, on whose brow, in whose eye,
Shone beauty and pleasure,—her triumphs are by ;
And the memory of those who loved her and praised,
Are alike from the minds of the living erased.

The hand of the king that the sceptre hath borne,
The brow of the priest that the mitre hath worn,

The eye of the sage and the heart of the brave,
Are hidden and lost in the depths of the grave.

The peasant, whose lot was to sow and to reap,
The herdsman, who climbed with his goats up the steep,
The beggar, who wandered in search of his bread,
Have faded away like the grass that we tread.

The saint, who enjoyed the communion of Heaven.
The sinner, who dared to remain unforgiven,
The wise and the foolish, the guilty and just,
Have quietly mingled their bones in the dust.

So the multitude goes—like the flower or the weed
That withers away to let others succeed;
So the multitude comes—even those we behold,
To repeat every tale that has often been told.

For we are the same our fathers have been;
We see the same sights our fathers have seen;
We drink the same stream, we view the same sun,
And run the same course our fathers have run.

The thoughts we are thinking our fathers would think;
From the death we are shrinking, our fathers would shrink
To the life we are clinging, they also would cling,—
But it speeds from us all like a bird on the wing.

They loved—but the story we can not unfold;
They scorned—but the heart of the haughty is cold;
They grieved—but no wail from their slumber will come
They joyed—but the tongue of their gladness is dumb.

They died—ay, they died; we things that are now,
That walk on the turf that lies over their brow,

And make in their dwellings a transient abode,
Meet the things that they met on their pilgrimage road.

'Tis the wink of an eye—'tis the draught of a breath—
From the blossom of health to the paleness of death,
From the gilded saloon to the bier and the shroud :—
Oh ! why should the spirit of mortal be proud ?

The last stanza will call to mind the startling suddenness with which Abraham Lincoln, the Chief Magistrate of a great nation, passed from the summit of power to the solemn stillness of death. Was it a sad, prophetic instinct that caused the mind of the great martyr to dwell so constantly upon these solemn strains ?

No man seems to have been more clearly indicated as the instrument of Providence than Abraham Lincoln. It seems strange in the eyes of men that a rough youth, born and reared in the backwoods, without early educational advantages, homely and awkward, and with no polish of manner save that which proceeded from a good heart, should have been selected as the Guide and Savior of a great nation. But God's ways are not as our ways, nor is His choice as ours. Mr. Lincoln had this advantage,—coming from the ranks of the people, he never lost sight of his sympathy for his class. His nature and his sympathies were broad and unconfined.

He has been well described by one reared like himself, in the free atmosphere of the West: "Nearly every great figure of history is a kind of great monstrosity. We know nothing about Washington. He is a steel engraving. No dirt of humanity clings to his boots. Lincoln lived where men were free and equal, and was acquainted with the people, not much with books. Every man is in some sort a book. He lived the poem of the year in the fields, the woods, the blessed country. Lincoln had the advantage of sociability. He was thoughtful, and saw on the horizon of his future the perpetual star of hope. To him every field was a landscape; every landscape a poem; every poem a lesson, and every grove a fairy land. Oaks and elms are far more poetical than streets or houses. A country life is in itself an education. It gives the man an idea of home. He hears the rain on the roofs, the rustle of the breeze, the music of nature's fullest control. You have no idea how many men education spoils. Lincoln's education was derived from men and things, and hence he had a chance to develop.

He had many sides. He not only had laughter, but he had tears, and never that kind of solemnity which is a wash to hide the features. He was not afraid to seek for knowledge where he had it not. When a man is too dignified he ceases to earn. He was always honest with himself. He was an orator; that is, he was natural. If you wish to be sublime you must keep close to the grass. You must sit close to the heart of human experience—above the clouds it is too cold. If you want to know the difference between an orator and a speaker read the oration of Lincoln at Gettysburg, and then read the speech of Everett at the same place. One came from the heart, the other was from out of the voice. Lincoln's speech will be remembered forever. Everett's no man will read. It was like plucked flowers.

"If you want to find out what a man is to the bottom, give him power. Any man can stand adversity—only a great man can stand prosperity. It is the glory of Abraham Lincoln that he never abused power only on the side of mercy. When he had power he used it in mercy. He loved to see the tears of the wife whose husband he had snatched from death."

I draw near the close of my task, having given, as I hope, some fair idea of one whose memory will always remain dear to the hearts of his countrymen. In that chequered life there is much to imitate, much to admire, little to avoid or censure. Happy will be the day when our public men copy his unselfishness, his patriotic devotion to duty!

Within a few months, on the eighteenth anniversary of Mr. Lincoln's assassination, a poem was read at his grave by John H. Bryant, of Princeton, which will fitly close my story of the Backwoods Boy:

> Not one of all earth's wise and great
> Hath earned a purer gratitude
> Than the great Soul whose hallowed dust
> This structure holds in sacred trust.
>
> How fierce the strife that rent the land,
> When he was summoned to command;
> With what wise care he led us through
> The fearful storms that 'round us blew.
>
> Calm, patient, hopeful, undismayed,
> He met the angry hosts arrayed
> For bloody war, and overcame
> Their haughty power in Freedom's name.
>
> 'Mid taunts and doubts, the bondsman's chain
> With gentle force he cleft in twain.

And raised four million slaves to be
The chartered sons of Liberty.

No debt he owed to wealth or birth ;
By force of solid, honest worth
He climbed the topmost height of fame
And wrote thereon a spotless name.

Oh ! when the felon hand laid low
That sacred head, what sudden woe
Shot to the Nation's farthest bound,
And every bosom felt the wound.

Well might the Nation bow in grief,
And weep above the fallen chief,
Who ever strove, by word or pen,
For " peace on earth, good-will to men."

The people loved him, for they knew,
Each pulse of his large heart was true
To them, to Freedom, and the right,
Unswayed by gain, unawed by might.

This tomb, by loving hands up-piled,
To him, the merciful and mild,
From age to age shall carry down
The glory of his great renown.

As the long centuries onward flow,
As generations come and go,
Wide and more wide his fame shall spread,
And greener laurels crown his head.

And when this pile is fall'n to dust,
'ts bronzes crumbled into rust,

Thy name, O Lincoln ' still shall be
Revered and loved from ꞏea to sea.

India's swart millions, 'neath their palms,
Shall sing thy praise in grateful psalms,
And crowds by Congo's turbid wave
Bless the good hand that freed the slave.

Shine on, O Star of Freedom, shine,
Till all the realms of earth are thine;
And all the tribes, through countless days,
Shall bask in thy benignant rays.

Lord of the Nations ! grant us still
Another patriot sage, to fill
The seat of power, and save the State
From selfish greed.   For this we wait.

THE
MAGNET LIBRARY

Of Fascinating Detective Stories

PUBLISHED EVERY WEEK

THIS line has become famous for its excellent stories of the detection of crime. Of late, it has taken truly remarkable strides in the public's favor. The reason for this is, that every book is a marvel of its kind. They are high-class tales, not of the "blood and thunder" order, but with plausible plots which hold the reader fairly captivated with breathless expectation. Among these are the stories of the adventures of Nick Carter and his clever assistants, of "Old Spicer," the clever private detective, whose exploits are among the most remarkable ever performed by any detective. If you are in search of good, interesting matter, a decided change from that to which you have been accustomed, purchase a few of these titles. They will not only please and interest you, but will give you a clear insight into the methods of the various classes of criminals.

THE MAGNET LIBRARY

The Harkaway Library

THIS line contains, exclusively, the exciting adventures of Jack Harkaway, now for the first time offered to our boys in low-priced edition.

Bracebridge Hemyng, the author, has established an enviable reputation. No better stories of adventure in school and out, on land and sea, have ever been written. The boy reader at once feels a most lively interest in Jack's welfare and desires to follow him through all the adventures that he experienced.

The following is a list of the titles now ready and those scheduled for early publication.

To be Published During June

20—Jack Harkaway in Australia......By Bracebridge Hemyng
19—Jack Harkaway's Resolve.........By Bracebridge Hemyng
18—Jack Harkaway's Pluck...........By Bracebridge Hemyng
17—Jack Harkaway in Greece........By Bracebridge Hemyng

To be Published During May

16—Jack Harkaway and the Red Dragon,
By Bracebridge Hemyng
15—Jack Harkaway in China..........By Bracebridge Hemyng
14—Jack Harkaway's Perils...........By Bracebridge Hemyng
13—Jack Harkaway in America.......By Bracebridge Hemyng

12—Jack Harkaway Around the World.By Bracebridge Hemyng
11—Jack Harkaway's Return..........By Bracebridge Hemyng
10—Jack Harkaway's Capture........By Bracebridge Hemyng
9—Jack Harkaway Among the Brigands,
By Bracebridge Hemyng
8—Jack Harkaway's Triumphs.......By Bracebridge Hemyng
7—Jack Harkaway's Struggles.......By Bracebridge Hemyng
6—Jack Harkaway at Oxford........By Bracebridge Hemyng
5—Jack Harkaway Among the Pirates.By Bracebridge Hemyng
4—Jack Harkaway Afloat and Ashore.By Bracebridge Hemyng
3—Jack Harkaway After School Days.By Bracebridge Hemyng
2—Jack Harkaway's Friends........By Bracebridge Hemyng
1—Jack Harkaway's School Days....By Bracebridge Hemyng

The New - - -
Secret Service Series

Published - Every - Week

A NEW line of high-class copyrighted stories, detailing principally the adventures of men of brain and muscle employed by our Government to ferret out and prevent federal crimes. These sleuths are stationed in every city, and the zeal which they display in the pursuit of their vocation, is nothing short of marvelous. In many instances, the stories in which these detectives figure are based upon their actual experiences. There are tales of Treasury and Mail robberies, Counterfeiting and Anarchists' plots and Smuggling. They are of such fascinating interest that it is indeed a pleasure to read them.

www.ingramcontent.com/pod-product-compliance
Lightning Source LLC
Chambersburg PA
CBHW060537030726
47498CB00004B/1232